ck

10662420

The Case
of the
Missing
Minds

ACCELERATED READER

LEVEL 4.1 _____

POINTS 3 _____

QUIZ 42361 _____

Three Rivers Regional
Library System
Gilchrist County Public Library
105 NE 11th Street
Trenton, FL 32693
3riverslibrary.com

Bethany House Books by
Bill Myers

Journeys to Fayrah
CHILDREN'S ALLEGORICAL SERIES

> *The Portal*
> *The Experiment*
> *The Whirlwind*
> *The Tablet*

Bloodhounds, Inc.
CHILDREN'S MYSTERY SERIES

> *The Ghost of KRZY*
> *The Mystery of the Invisible Knight*
> *Phantom of the Haunted Church*
> *Invasion of the UFOs*
> *Fangs for the Memories*
> *The Case of the Missing Minds*

Nonfiction

> *The Dark Side of the Supernatural*
> *Hot Topics, Tough Questions*

6

BloodHounds, INC.

The Case of the Missing Minds

Bill Myers

BETHANY HOUSE PUBLISHERS
MINNEAPOLIS, MINNESOTA 55438

The Case of the Missing Minds
Copyright © 1999
Bill Myers

Cover illustration by Joe Nordstrom
Cover design by the Lookout Design Group

Unless otherwise identified, Scripture quotations are from the HOLY BIBLE, NEW INTERNATIONAL VERSION®. Copyright © 1973, 1978, 1984 by International Bible Society. Used by permission of Zondervan Publishing House. All rights reserved. The "NIV" and "New International Version" trademarks are registered in the United States Patent and Trademark Office by International Bible Society. Use of either trademark requires the permission of International Bible Society.

All rights reserved. No part of this publication may be reproduced, stored in a retrieval system, or transmitted in any form or by any means—electronic, mechanical, photocopying, recording, or otherwise—without the prior written permission of the publisher and copyright owners.

Published by Bethany House Publishers
A Ministry of Bethany Fellowship International
11400 Hampshire Avenue South
Minneapolis, Minnesota 55438
www.bethanyhouse.com

Printed in the United States of America by
Bethany Press International, Minneapolis, Minnesota 55438

Library of Congress Cataloging-in-Publication Data

Myers, Bill, 1953–
    The case of the missing minds / by Bill Myers ; with David Wimbish.
       p. cm. — (Bloodhounds, Inc. ; 6)
    Summary: When a visiting troupe hypnotizes some of the people of Midvale and a mysterious string of robberies ensues, Sean and Melissa use their detective skills to find the thief.
    ISBN 1–55661–490-X (pbk.)
    [1. Hypnotism Fiction. 2. Brothers and sisters Fiction. 3. Christian life Fiction. 4. Mystery and detective stories.] I. Wimbish, David. II. Title.
III. Series: Myers, Bill, 1953–   Bloodhounds, Inc. ; 6.
PZ7.M98234Cas   1999   99–6474
[Fic]—dc21   CIP

Three Rivers Regional
Library System
Gilchrist County Public Library
105 NE 11th Street
Trenton, FL 32693
3riverslibrary.com

To Robert Elmer:

Another writer committed
to touching children's hearts.

BILL MYERS is a youth worker and creative writer and film director who co-created the "McGee and Me!" book and video series and whose work has received over forty national and international awards. His many youth books include THE INCREDIBLE WORLDS OF WALLY MCDOOGLE, JOURNEYS TO FAYRAH, as well as his teen books, *Hot Topics, Tough Questions* and *Forbidden Doors*.

Contents

*Take captive every thought
to make it obedient to Christ.*

2 Corinthians 10:5

1

The Case Begins

SATURDAY, 9:46 PDST

It wasn't the weirdest thing he had ever seen—but it was close. It looked kind of like a football helmet, but it was covered with electrodes, cathodes, and a dozen other types of *odes*, all sticking out at different angles.

Sean turned it over in his hands, studying its complicated design. Let's see. This button turned it on. This button increased the power. And this button? Hmm . . . no telling what this button did.

Yes, sir, from the looks of things, this might be Doc's number one, all-time best invention ever. Then again, it might wind up being just another weird thing collecting dust in the corner . . . which is what all of her other failed inventions had become.

It was a rare lazy Saturday morning for Sean and his

sister, Melissa, co-owners of the Bloodhounds, Incorporated Detective Agency. Most of the time there was a lot going on in Midvale, but the last couple of weeks had been pretty boring.

So along with their big bloodhound, Slobs, Sean and Melissa headed up to Doc's attic laboratory to see what she was working on. When they'd first met Doc, they'd thought she was a little bit strange . . . well, actually, a lot strange. And definitely not friendly. But what they thought was unfriendliness turned out to be something completely different.

Doc was deaf, which meant she didn't know when someone was talking to her or what they were saying unless she could read their lips. She couldn't speak, either, so when she had something to say, she usually typed it out on one of the many computer keyboards around the lab. Over time, Sean and Melissa had gotten so used to reading Doc's monitors that they'd almost forgotten she couldn't talk.

This afternoon, Doc had several new gadgets in the works, but Sean's attention was captured by the device he held in his hands. Doc called it a "thinking cap."

"Let me get this straight," Sean said. "If I put this thing on my head, it's supposed to make me smarter?"

Melissa bit her lip to keep from laughing, and Sean shot her a look. He knew what she was thinking: *It wouldn't take much to make* you *smarter*.

Meanwhile, Slobs had stood up on her hind legs to get a better view of the helmet. She stuck her nose between the diodes and started to sniff.

"Down, girl!" Sean ordered as he pulled the helmet away from her. "You're going to get drool all over it!" As you may have guessed, Slobs, which is short for Slobbers, did not get her name by accident.

Doc moved to her keyboard and typed:

> **Theoretically, the helmet should raise your IQ at least twenty points. But it hasn't been tested yet.**

"How's it work?" Melissa asked.

> **It focuses and strengthens the electrical energy produced by the brain. It's kind of like a radio tuner. At least, in theory.**

"Wow!" Sean looked at the weird-looking contraption again. "Just think what that would mean! No more studying! Just put the hat on, push a couple of buttons, and *bingo*, an instant A in algebra!"

Melissa only answered by rolling her eyes. She was an expert eye roller.

"How about letting me try it out?" Sean asked.

Doc thought for a moment and then typed:

11

It's not been proven. What if something goes wrong?

"What could possibly go wrong?" Sean asked. But instead of waiting for the answer, he pulled the strange-looking helmet onto his head and fastened the leather strap underneath his chin.

Slobs covered her eyes with her paws and whined loudly. Years of experience with Sean had taught her something bad was about to happen.

"Now what?" Sean asked.

Doc pointed at the button on the front of the helmet, then typed:

That knob turns it on.

"Like this?" Melissa reached over and gave it a slight twist.

Doc nodded and typed:

And that other button turns up the frequency. Be careful. Just a little bit.

Melissa turned the other knob, ever so slightly. Then she stepped back and waited. "Feel any smarter?" she asked.

"Not really," Sean answered. "Maybe you ought to turn it up some more."

"Okay." She gave it another twist. "Feel anything now?"

"Nothing."

Suddenly a voice crackled from Sean's wristwatch: "Well, you know what they say . . . if at first you don't succeed, try new batteries."

Sean glanced down to see a little leprechaun-like figure grinning up at him. "Hi, Jeremiah!"

"Actually," Melissa corrected good-naturedly, "I think the saying is, 'If at first you don't succeed, try, try again.'"

Jeremiah shrugged. "Yeah, that might work, too."

Jeremiah—which stood for Johnson Electronic Reductive Entity Memory Inductive Assembly Housing—was one of Doc's first and best inventions. He wasn't a real person. Or was he? He was made completely of electrical energy, but he had his own unique personality and intelligence. He loved to talk in proverbs and slogans, but ever since that time he got lost in a fortune-cookie factory computer, well, let's just say he can never quite get those sayings right.

Sean, Melissa, and Doc were the only three people who knew about Jeremiah, and they felt it was better to keep it that way. Frankly, the rest of the world wasn't ready for him. In fact, a lot of the time *they* weren't ready for him.

Because he was electronic, Jeremiah was able to go wherever electricity could go, which meant he could go just about anywhere. Often his "home" was Sean's digital watch. But sometimes he showed up on computer games at the arcade, on a television set . . . or anything else with a monitor or a viewing screen. Once or twice, when the air was charged with enough electricity, he had even managed to jump outside of his electrical universe and become a part of the "real world." And when that happened . . . look out!

Taking Jeremiah's advice, Melissa reached out and gave Sean's helmet another boost of power.

"Wait a minute!" Sean put his hands to his head. "I think . . . I think . . ."

"You think what?" Melissa encouraged.

"I think . . . that . . . for any right triangle, the square of the hypotenuse is equal to the sum of the square of the other two sides."

Melissa's mouth fell open. "Wow! That is so—"

"Shhh," her brother motioned for silence. "I just thought of something else! For any quadratic equation, the value of X is equal to the opposite of B plus or minus the square root of B squared minus four AC over two times A!"

It was about this time that Melissa noticed Sean was beginning to sweat. Reaching for the control knob, she said, "Maybe I ought to turn it down just a little—"

But Sean pushed her hand away. "Don't you dare!" Suddenly he burst out laughing. "Oh, of course, of course! Why didn't I see this before? Do you realize that for any function F at X, its derivative is equal to the limit as H approaches zero . . . F at X plus H minus F at X divided by H? Hey, wait a minute! I think I see where Einstein made his mistake!"

Again Melissa reached for the control knob. "I really think—"

"Power!" Sean shouted. "I need more power!" He grabbed the knob, and before Melissa or Doc could stop him, he turned it all the way to *HIGH*.

"Sean!" Melissa shouted. "Don't!"

Too late.

Sean clapped his hands together. "I've got it!" he yelled. "I've got it!"

"Got what?"

Sean didn't answer. Instead . . .

. . . his eyes bugged out . . .

. . . his teeth began to chatter and . . .

. . . his face turned bright red.

Sweat began streaming down his forehead.

"Sean!" Melissa cried. "Sean, are you all right?"

"Ga . . . ga . . . ga . . . ga . . . ga . . . ga . . ." came the answer.

Doc motioned frantically for Melissa to turn down the power. She grabbed the knob and twisted it hard. Too hard. So hard that it broke off in her hand. She turned back to Sean. Was that her imagination, or was smoke really coming out of her brother's ears?

"Ga . . . ga . . . ga . . . ga . . . ga . . . ga . . . !"

KA-BLAM!

And that's when Sean's head exploded! No . . . wait, it wasn't his head . . . it was only the helmet. One of the biggest cathode tubes flew off the helmet, like a rocket lifting off at Cape Canaveral. It . . .

K-RASHED!

. . . right through Doc's attic window and kept going until it . . .

S-MASHED!

. . . through the next-door neighbor's front door and . . .

K-RASH! TINKLE-TINKLE-TINKLE!

. . . came out through the neighbor's back window, still traveling a hundred miles an hour.

Unfortunately, that was the good news. The bad news was that the kids' crotchety neighbor, Mrs. Tubbs—who was always at the wrong place at the wrong time—just happened to be taking her fat, snobby cat, Precious, for a walk.

Neither of them saw it coming.

The rocket-powered cathode tube screamed out of the neighbor's window and landed right in the middle of Mrs. Tubbs' bouffant hairdo, which was piled high atop her head.

Doc's window hadn't been able to stop the tube. The neighbor's door hadn't been able to stop it. Their back window hadn't succeeded, either. But when it hit that stiff, hair-sprayed hairdo of Mrs. Tubbs, its flight was all over. The tube stayed there, completely stuck, sizzling and smoking.

"Augh!" Mrs. Tubbs screamed. "Help me! Somebody help me!"

Of course, Precious, startled by Mrs. Tubbs' screams (and all that smoke coming out of her hair) decided he'd better run for cover. And when that big cat decides to run, nothing stops him. Not even a woman with a leash wrapped several times around her hands.

"P-P-Precious . . . stop!" she shouted.

But Precious wasn't about to stop. He was taking the shortest path home, and he didn't care what stood in his way . . . even if it was Mr. Williams, who was busy painting his house with his electric-powered sprayer.

The cat ran easily under the man's legs. Mrs. Tubbs,

who was hanging on to the leash with one hand and frantically slapping at her smoking hair with the other, wasn't so lucky.

K-WHAP!

When she ran into Mr. Williams, he let go of the sprayer, which snaked across the front yard like a runaway garden hose, spewing white paint in all directions. Across the big living room window...

SPLISH!

... over Mrs. Williams' brand new car...

SPLASH!

... and finally...

SPLISH! SPLASH! SPLISH!
SPLASH! SPLISH! SPLASH!

... right in Mrs. Tubbs' face!

But even that didn't slow down Precious. He raced toward the backyard (still pulling Mrs. Tubbs behind) straight toward the clothesline where Mrs. Williams' laundry was hanging.

WHAP!

Well, where it *had* been hanging ... until Mrs. Tubbs

ran smack into the biggest sheet, which wrapped around her, causing her to stagger and spin in all directions. She waved her arms, shouting, "Help me! Help me!" (Of course, with that sheet wrapped around her face, it sounded more like, "Hoooeeeeee! Hooeeee!")

Next door, old Mr. Webster, who wasn't quite "right" these days (he had covered his TV set with a blanket because he thought Regis and Kathy Lee were spying on him) sat on his porch. He took one look at Mrs. Tubbs stumbling into his front yard and decided she was a ghost . . . which would explain why he raced into the house and came out with his 12-gauge shotgun blasting away.

K-BAMB! K-BAMB!

The first shot destroyed his mailbox. The second missed everything, but it scared Mrs. Tubbs so badly that she finally let go of Precious's leash. She dove for cover and . . .

K-WHAP!

. . . landed stomach-first on Billy Williams' skateboard . . . which shot off down the sidewalk with her on it.

"HOOOEEEE . . ."

She picked up speed as she raced down the steep hill.

"HOOOEEEE!"

Just ahead, two delivery men were unloading a giant big-screen TV from their truck. When they heard her scream, they looked up, then tried to get out of the way. Unfortunately, one ran one way, the other, another . . . which meant the TV had no place to go but . . .

K-SMASH-TINKLE-CRASH!

. . . onto the sidewalk.

But Mrs. Tubbs' tour of Midvale wasn't entirely over . . . not yet.

WHACK!

There went another mailbox.

WHACK!

Make that *two* mailboxes.

Next, she bounced off the sidewalk and whizzed past the stop sign . . . right into the middle of busy Fifth Street.

SCREEEEECH!

One car skidded to miss her and ran up on the sidewalk hitting a fire hydrant, which shot a powerful stream of water high into the air.

Another car swerved directly into the path of an oncoming garbage truck.

Luckily, the truck had excellent brakes.

SQUEEEEEL!

Not so lucky was the fact that it was filled with garbage, which spilled all over the street when it skidded to a halt.

But none of this stopped Mrs. Tubbs, who zipped right underneath the big truck and out the other side . . . not, of course, without picking up a thick layer of rotten banana peels, coffee grounds, and chicken bones along the way.

When she hit the curb at the other end of the intersection, the skateboard finally came to a stop. But not Mrs. Tubbs. She went flying through the air all on her own.

Thankfully—or maybe not so thankfully—Mr. Snyder had just finished pouring concrete for his brand-new driveway. He was just pounding a Caution! Wet Cement sign into the ground as Mrs. Tubbs sailed over his head and finally . . .

K-PLOP!

. . . did a magnificent belly flop right in the middle of the man's handiwork.

21

The good news was she had finally come to a stop.
The bad news was she wasn't exactly happy.

SATURDAY, 10:02 PDST

Meanwhile, back in Doc's attic, Sean's cell phone

BRREP! BRREP!

began to ring.

He pulled it out of his pocket and answered:
"Bloodhounds, Incorporated."

"Sean Hunter, please."

"Speaking."

"Who is it?" Melissa asked.

Sean waved for her to be silent.

"My name is Sam Maxwell. I own the Midvale
Comedy Club. I have a little problem, and I thought
maybe you could help me out."

"What kind of problem?"

"Well . . ." Mr. Maxwell hesitated a moment. "It's
kind of . . . uh . . . weird."

"Weirdness is our specialty," Sean assured him. "Go
on."

"Someone's been stealing money from our cash
register."

"That's not really so unusual," Sean said.

"There's more to it than that. One moment the money's in the drawer, the next moment it's gone. I mean, I open the drawer, put the money in; then I open it again, and it's missing."

"That *is* weird," Sean agreed.

Maxwell continued. "Some of my employees are scared. They're threatening to quit. They think . . . well, they think the place is haunted."

2

Sad Comedy

SATURDAY, 13:15 PDST

BANG! BANG! BANG!

"Cut it out!" Melissa cried. "Honestly, sometimes you can be so impatient!"

Sean ignored her and kept beating on the bathroom door.

BANG! BANG! BANG!

"Hurry up, will you! We're gonna be late!"

"Just a minute!" she shouted back.

"That's what you said *thirty* minutes ago!"

Melissa frowned at the mirror and thought, *Why does my hair have to pick today to look this way?* Suddenly she stuck her tongue out at her reflection.

"Misty!" Sean shouted. He raised his fist for another

round of door pounding, when she suddenly opened the door and he stumbled into the room nearly falling into the bathtub.

"You expect me to go like this?" she complained.

"Like what?" he asked as he got back to his feet.

"Look at my hair! And don't you roll your eyes at me!"

"You're the eye-rolling expert!" he said. "And your hair looks fine. Now, for crying out loud, let's go!"

Melissa took another glance in the mirror. "My hair does *not* look fine! I look like I just stuck my finger in an electric socket!"

"That's how it always looks."

"Sean!" She shoved him out of the bathroom, slammed the door, and locked it behind him. "Jerk!"

"No . . . listen . . . I didn't mean . . ." He sighed heavily, then tried another tactic. "Misty, you really look great! Honest! Now, come on out of there and—"

"What's all the commotion?" Dad called as he headed up the stairs. He'd just come home from another Saturday morning working at the radio station he owned.

"Oh, hi, Dad," Sean said, putting on a smile. "Nothing, really. Just that—"

Melissa jerked open the door and shouted, "He said my hair looks like I stuck my finger in an electric socket!"

Sean slapped his forehead with his hand in make-believe shock. "Me? Me make such an unkind remark about my beautiful sister?"

"Don't you dare lie about it, Sean Hunter!"

Before things got too out of control, Dad arrived and gently put his hand on Melissa's shoulder. "Well, even if he did say it—"

"But I didn't!" Sean interrupted.

"Or even if you *thought* he said it," Dad continued, "it's not true. You look beautiful, Misty."

"I do?"

"Yes, you do."

Melissa smiled, ran her hands through her hair one last time, then floated past her father and brother toward the stairs. "Well, come on, Sean," she called over her shoulder. "You don't want to be late, do you?"

Sean could only stare, then shake his head in amazement. Sisters, go figure.

"So," Dad asked as he followed them back down the stairs, "where exactly are you two headed today?"

Sean started to answer. "We've got a case over at—"

"The comedy club," Melissa interrupted as she checked her hair again in the mirror over the fireplace. "And they gave us tickets to this afternoon's show."

"Show?" Dad asked. "What kind of show?"

Sean shrugged. "I don't know. Comedy, I guess."

Always eager to correct her brother, Melissa chimed in, "It's a couple of guys who hypnotize people and get them to act like dogs and cats, and—"

"How'd you know that?" Sean asked.

"You'd know, too," she sniffed, "if you ever read the newspaper. But then again, you're not much better at reading than you are at math, are you?"

"Thank you, Miss Electric Socket," Sean said.

Melissa spun around and started at her brother until Dad stepped between them. "That's enough, now. If you two can't get along any better than that, then maybe you shouldn't be going anywhere."

Knowing Dad meant business, Sean suddenly turned on the charm. "I'm sorry, dearest sister. You know I love you," he cooed.

"Oh, and I love you, too, dear brother," she cooed back.

Dad groaned good-naturedly. "I think I'm going to be sick. Look, all I'm saying is be nice to each other, okay?"

"Okay," they agreed. "We will."

"Now, you say this show's about hypnotism?" Dad asked.

"Yeah," Melissa answered.

A frown appeared on Dad's forehead.

"Is there something wrong with that?" Sean asked.

The frown grew deeper. "I'm not sure. But God's

pretty clear about not giving anyone control over our minds."

"Does the Bible say hypnotism is wrong?" Melissa asked.

Dad shook his head. "No, not in so many words. But it does tell us that we need to be careful what we think . . . and that our thoughts should be under God's control, not anybody else's."

As they started toward the door, he continued. "I've also read that the hypnotic state is like the trance mediums go into when they claim to speak to the dead. And we've already discussed what God feels about that."

"He hates it," Sean said.

"Yes, He does," Dad agreed. "So please . . . be careful."

"We will, Dad," Melissa promised. "But . . ."

"But what?"

"Well, sometimes I wish we *could* talk to the dead."

Dad pulled her close and kissed the top of her head. "Nobody misses your mother more than I do, sweetheart. Someday we'll all be with her in heaven. But until then, we just have to wait."

Melissa nodded. She could feel the back of her throat tightening with emotion. It had been nearly a year since they'd lost Mom to cancer, and even though the pain was slowly fading, the emptiness never seemed to leave.

"Sometimes . . ." Melissa took a deep breath and continued. "Sometimes heaven seems so far away. I just wish I could talk to her now."

"So do I," Dad whispered quietly. "So do I."

SATURDAY, 15:18 PDST

The audience howled with laughter.

Up on stage, Midvale's tough chief of police, John Robertson, was acting like a chicken. Well, a rooster, to be exact. He strutted around the stage, pawing at the floor with his feet. Then he paused, turned his head toward the audience, and let loose with a perfect *"COCK-A-DOODLE-DOO!"*

He puffed his chest out proudly and went back to pawing the ground.

One of the two hypnotists, a man named Larry, moved toward the chief and pointed at the floor. "Chief, look!" he shouted. "A worm!"

The chief flapped his arms excitedly and began searching frantically for the tasty worm. But when Larry moved close to him and calmly said the words "Chocolate Cake," the chief immediately stopped acting like a rooster. Instead, he stood still, staring out at the audience.

Larry, a tall, distinguished man with silver hair and a

mustache, was the obvious star of the show. He was wearing a perfectly tailored blue suit with a color-coordinated handkerchief neatly tucked into the top pocket of his jacket. "Ladies and gentlemen," he said, "I want you to meet my partner. The man who introduced me to the magic of hypnotism. The one . . . the only . . . Zomar the Magnificent!"

A small white spotlight shone into the auditorium, where a man stood in the middle of the audience, holding a microphone.

Sean leaned toward his sister and whispered, "Zomar the Magnificent. Now, that sounds like a hypnotist!"

"Yeah," Melissa agreed. "A lot more impressive than . . . 'Larry'!"

But he sure didn't look as impressive. In fact, as the lights came up, he was every bit as rumpled and sloppy as Larry was distinguished. He was heavy and short, and with his striped tie and checkered suit, it looked like he'd picked his clothes out in the dark.

Zomar the Magnificent bowed deeply to the audience. Then he thrust his microphone into the face of the man sitting next to him. "Sir, tell us your name and where you're from."

"Uh . . . I'm Herbie, and I'm from right here in Midvale."

"And, Herbie, what do you do for a living?"

"I'm an engineer for radio station KRZY."

Sean winked at his sister. This ought to be good! Herbie was their father's chief engineer. Well, actually, he was the *only* engineer. He was the nicest, most friendly guy you'd ever want to meet. But he wasn't exactly the intellectual type. He'd be hopping around on stage like a chicken in no time!

"Herbie, come up on stage!" said Zomar the Magnificent.

As the people clapped, Herbie raced to the front.

Meanwhile, Zomar worked his way through the audience looking for more victims . . . er . . . volunteers. He stopped in front of someone sitting a few rows away. "And how about you, young man? What's your name?"

"Spalding" came the reply.

"Well, Spalding, how would you like to be a star?"

Melissa leaned over to Sean. "This ought to be even better than Herbie."

Sean nodded and they both laughed. As the only child of the richest man in town, Spalding was spoiled, selfish, and a world-class snob. It would be great to see him make a fool of himself.

Next up was Mrs. Applewhite, Sean's math teacher.

He shook his head when he saw her stiffly making her way up on stage. "They'll never get through to her," Sean told Melissa. "That woman is all brains."

Melissa nodded and glanced to the back of the room where they were keeping an eye on the cash register. So far, so good. No one was trying to steal anything. Of course, with Chief Robertson hanging around, it was doubtful they'd try, even if the chief wasn't exactly himself this afternoon.

Up on stage, Herbie, Spalding, and Mrs. Applewhite sat in folding chairs while Larry talked quietly with them.

Whispering into his microphone, Zomar the Magnificent explained to the audience what was happening. "Larry is putting each of these people into a light hypnotic trance. There is absolutely no danger. When they are in the trance, they will be peaceful and relaxed. When Larry brings them out of it, they will feel terrific!"

Melissa turned to take another look at the cash register. As she did, she noticed the time on the big wall clock.

Three-thirty and all is well, she thought.

Back on stage, Larry turned to Herbie and said the word *pie*. Instantly the big, clumsy Herbie began meowing like a kitty. Zomar tossed a rubber mouse onto the floor, and Herbie dropped to his hands and knees, happily batting it around as everyone laughed and applauded.

33

Meanwhile, Larry stood behind Spalding, with his hands on the boy's shoulders. "Uh-oh!" he said. "Here comes trouble! Spalding, do you know what you are?"

Spalding shook his head.

"When I say the word *pie*, you'll become a dog. A great big German shepherd. Do you understand?"

Spalding nodded.

"Pie!" Larry shouted.

Suddenly Spalding's tongue dropped out of his mouth and he began panting.

"And you know what you hate?"

Immediately, he replied, "WOOF! WOOF!"

"That's right," said Larry. "You hate cats! And there's one right now!" He pointed at Herbie.

"GRRRRR! WOOF! WOOF!"
"MEOWRRRR!! HISSSSSS!"

Herbie took off with Spalding yapping and snapping at him all the way. The audience laughed so loud, they practically roared as the little boy chased the big man around and around on the stage. Everyone was having a great time . . . well, everyone but Mrs. Applewhite. She sat quietly in her chair, staring straight ahead, waiting for her moment in the spotlight.

It came before she expected it. Little Kitty Herbie was looking for someone to protect him from Big Dog

Spalding. That's when he spotted Mrs. Applewhite. He was a good six feet from her when he leaped high into the air and . . .

"OOOOOF!"

. . . landed directly in her lap . . . all two hundred pounds of Kitty Herbie! Unfortunately, when he landed on her, the chair collapsed, and . . .

K-RASH!

. . . the two of them hit the floor!

The loud commotion scared Big Dog Spalding, who ran to the corner of the stage, yelping and yapping, looking for a place to hide.

But the show wasn't over yet. Not quite.

When Larry ran to help Mrs. Applewhite up, he whispered something into her ear and then, more loudly, said, "Pie!"

Immediately, she pushed him away. "Get your hands off me!" she commanded. "Just who do you think you are?"

"That's not really important," Larry said. "But why don't you tell me—and all of these nice people here—who *you* are." He winked at the audience.

"Humph," Mrs. Applewhite said. "I hardly think that's necessary. I can't go anywhere without being

35

recognized. Everyone knows the great ballerina . . . *Tutu Frutu!*"

More laughter from the audience.

"So tell me, Tutu Frutu," Zomar said, "will you dance for us?"

"Oh yes . . . I was born to dance!" Then Mrs. Applewhite, who was even bigger than Herbie, began swaying back and forth, listening to the music in her head. Suddenly she began dancing across the stage on her tiptoes. She twirled, she kicked, she pirouetted. The sight was hilarious.

Melissa was having a great time and didn't want the show to end. She absent-mindedly glanced at her watch. *Four-thirty! Good grief? It seems like five minutes ago it was 3:30! Where did the hour go?*

Was there a problem with her watch? She turned and looked at the clock on the back wall. It, too, said 4:30!

Wow! she thought. *Time really does fly when you're having fun.*

Up on stage, Zomar the Magnificent and Larry were about to bring their subjects out of their trances.

"When you hear the words *chocolate cake*," Zomar shouted, "you will wake up feeling rested and refreshed. One . . . two . . . three . . . Chocolate Cake!"

Suddenly Chief Robertson, Spalding, Mrs. Applewhite, and Herbie were all back to their normal selves, and the audience responded with loud applause.

As the cheers died down, Larry raised his hand to ask for silence. "Thank you for being such a great audience!" he said. "We've had a lot of fun this afternoon, and we hope you have, too!"

More whistling and applause. For some reason, Zomar had pulled Herbie toward the back and was speaking quietly to him as Larry continued. "But hypnotism is more than just a comedy act. It's a great way to help you deal with personal problems. It can help you quit smoking, lose weight, sleep better at night." He paused for effect. "And one of the very best ways hypnotism can help is to take you back in time . . . to the days before you were born . . . and help you discover who you were in your past lives."

"Past lives?" Melissa whispered. "This is getting kind of weird."

"Yeah," Sean replied. "Is he talking about reincarnation?"

"You see," Larry continued, "the things that happened to you in your past lives are going to make a difference in this one. Only by knowing who you were then can you be at peace with who you are now.

"Right now, Zomar the Magnificent is taking our friend Herbie back into one of his past lives, just to demonstrate the process for you."

Zomar and Herbie now walked slowly to the front of the stage.

"My friend," Zomar said to Herbie. "What year is it?"

"It's 1882," Herbie said.

The audience gasped.

"And why don't you tell these fine people who you are."

"Why, I'm the rootin-tootinest, fastest-shootinest feller who ever strapped on a six-gun, that's who I am."

"Which means you are . . ."

Herbie reached into an imaginary holster, pulled out an imaginary revolver, and pointed it at Zomar's head.

"What's the matter with you?" he demanded. "You don't recognize Jesse James?"

"Jesse James?"

"The one and only. And here're the other members of my gang." He pointed to Spalding. "That there is Frank, my brother, and over there"—he pointed to Mrs. Applewhite—"is my sister, Pauline. Hey, wait a minute, is that a sheriff?" He was looking right at Chief Robertson.

"Actually," the chief cleared his throat. "I'm a police officer and—"

"A policeman!" Herbie shouted. "Then I gotta get out of here!" He jumped off the stage and ran toward the exit.

"Chocolate Cake!" Zomar shouted. Immediately, Herbie stopped running and stood still.

"Folks," Larry said, "this was not an act. Herbie actually was Jesse James in a past life. And once he figures out what that means for him, then he'll do a better job of facing the problems he has in this life. The same is true of you! That's why we've opened a hypnotherapy office right here in Midvale. We're located at 1513 West Main Street, and we're available for appointments Monday through Friday from 9:00 A.M. until 5:00 P.M."

"Come see us," said Zomar the Magnificent. "Hypnotism can improve your life. We guarantee it!"

"Good-bye, now!" shouted Larry. "You've been a great audience."

After more cheering and applause, the house lights came up.

Melissa and Sean joined the happy crowd as they slowly made their way to the back of the Comedy Club. Sam Maxwell stood waiting for them near the ticket counter.

"So," he asked, "did you two see anything unusual this afternoon?"

"No, sir," Melissa shook her head. "Nothing at all. I mean, except for what went on up on the stage."

Sean nodded and, never suffering from too little

pride, added, "Maybe whoever's been stealing your money found out we were going to be here and ran for cover."

Melissa rolled her eyes. Was there any end to her big brother's ego? "The point is," she said, "the money from today's show is right in that cash register where it belongs."

Maxwell nodded in agreement and reached over to open the cash register's drawer. That's when his eyes grew wide in shock. "What?!" he shouted.

Melissa leaned past him and saw it, too. "Sean!" she cried. "Sean, it's gone!"

"What's gone?"

"The cash register! It's . . . completely empty!"

3

Does Anybody Really Know What Time It Is?

SATURDAY, 17:27 PDST

Sean and Melissa sat on the curb with their heads in their hands.

"How in the world. . . ?" Sean began.

"I don't know."

"But I didn't see anybody. . . ."

"Neither did I."

"And I kept my eye on the cash register."

"So did I," Melissa said. "No wonder Mr. Maxwell's employees think it's a ghost. But why would a ghost need money?"

Sean shook his head. "This talk about ghosts isn't getting us anywhere. I think this has to be an inside job."

"Meaning?"

"Meaning that one of Mr. Maxwell's employees is

stealing the money. I don't know how he's doing it . . . but that's the only logical explanation."

"So what do we do now?"

"We're going to have to think of a way to catch him in the act."

The two young detectives sat in silence for a few moments, wondering what their next move should be.

All along the sidewalks of Main Street, local farmers were setting up their booths for the farmer's market, which took place in Midvale every Saturday night. The street was closed to traffic between 6:00 and 10:00 P.M., when hundreds of people crowded the area looking for bargains on fresh fruits and vegetables.

Sean sighed again. "Well, I guess we'd better head on home. Seeing all this food is starting to make me hungry." He glanced at his watch and shook his head. "Man, this day went by fast, didn't it?"

"That's just what I've been thinking," Melissa answered.

Suddenly Jeremiah's image appeared on Sean's digital watch. He looked even weirder than usual—which was something. He had a huge, silly grin on his face. His eyes were open wide, and he seemed to be staring at something off in the distance.

"Jeremiah," Sean asked, "you okay?"

But Jeremiah didn't answer. He just kept on smiling,

changing colors as energy pulsed through him—from red to purple to blue to green to yellow to orange and then back to red.

"Did you catch any of the show?" Sean asked.

The electronic leprechaun opened his mouth and answered, "Doo-a-doodle cock!"

Then he began pecking at the face of Sean's watch with his nose.

"Jeremiah, what are you doing!?"

"DOO-A-DOODLE COCK!"

Sean glanced at his sister. Jeremiah, who was obviously pretending to be a rooster, couldn't even say those words correctly. Wait a minute. That last crowing didn't come from the watch. It came from . . . behind. Slowly, Sean turned to face the store they were sitting in front of—Miller's Electronics. As usual, the display window was full of VCRs and TV screens. But this time Jeremiah's face was staring out from each and every one of those screens.

"What's he doing?!" Melissa urgently whispered.

Sean rose to his feet and answered, "I think we have a problem. . . ."

SATURDAY, 17:35 PDST

Back inside the Comedy Club, Larry was arguing with Sam Maxwell.

"I can't believe this!" he shouted. "This makes four shows in a row you haven't paid us a penny!" He was so angry that his face was red, and the veins on the side of his neck were bulging.

"Please," Maxwell pleaded, "be patient. I'm doing my best to find out what's going on here. I promise, you'll get your money."

"We'd better!" Larry angrily poked his finger into Maxwell's chest.

Zomar the Magnificent walked up quietly and put his hand on his partner's shoulder.

"Calm down, Larry," he said. "You look like you're about to have a stroke."

"Calm down? This man owes us nearly $3,000!"

"But it's not his fault."

"Obviously, the man has a lousy security system. And if he doesn't pay us what he owes us, I'm going to sue."

Maxwell put his hands up in a pleading gesture. "Please, that won't be necessary. You'll get your money."

"Easy, Larry," Zomar said. "We've got to be more trust—"

Larry angrily knocked Zomar's hand off his shoulder

and turned to Maxwell. "If we don't get our money by this time next week, you'll be hearing from our attorney!"

He spun around and stormed off.

Zomar watched him go, then turned back to Maxwell. "I'm sorry," he said. "I know this is hard for you, too. I'll try to calm him down."

Maxwell sighed. "I just don't know what's going on. Maybe they're right. Maybe the place really is haunted!"

SATURDAY, 17:41 PDST

"DOO-A-DOODLE COCK!"

Jeremiah's voice rang out from a dozen television screens.

"Don't look now," Melissa whispered, "but people are starting to notice."

"Starting to notice?" Sean said. "How could they *not* notice?"

Sure enough, a crowd had gathered in front of the electronics store, pointing and laughing as Jeremiah strutted around, flapping his arms like an overgrown electronic chicken.

"What in the world is that?" someone asked.

"I think it's a new sitcom," someone else answered.

45

"Wow!" another said. "The shows are really getting better, aren't they?"

Sean leaned over to Melissa and whispered, "We've got to do something before this gets out of hand."

"But what? Why is Jeremiah acting so crazy?"

"Beats me."

Melissa glanced around to make sure no one was paying attention to them. She didn't have to worry. Every eye of the growing crowd was staring at Jeremiah.

Inside the store, a salesman frantically changed channels on all of the store's TV sets. It didn't matter. Jeremiah remained on every screen.

Sean began pushing buttons on his digital watch, trying to get through to his electronic friend. But nothing worked. "Jeremiah," he whispered. "Listen to me! You've got to stop this. You're going to get us all in trouble!"

"DOO-A-DOODLE COCK!"

"Boy," a man in the crowd shouted. "The idea for this show is cool, but the writing sure stinks!"

"Yeah," a woman agreed. "All he does is walk around flapping his arms and crowing like a rooster. When is something exciting going to happen?"

She shouldn't have asked.

The picture on the television screens hiccuped momentarily, then went blank. The next moment, all the TV sets in the store were back to normal. Five were tuned to silly sitcoms, three to sleazy talk shows, and two to infomercials.

"Hey!" the first man shouted. "Bring back that rooster guy!"

"Yeah! His show was better than this junk!"

"DOO-A-DOODLE COCK!!"

But the voice was no longer coming from the TV sets. Now it was coming from above. The entire crowd tilted back their heads and looked up.

"DOO-A-DOODLE COCK!"

"AUGH!" they screamed. "It's a monster!"

Yes, it was a monster. An electronic monster named Jeremiah! He towered over them, five or six stories high. If anyone had taken the time to really look, they would have seen that he was just a holographic image. But they were too busy screaming and running for their lives to notice such details.

"DOO-A-DOODLE COCK!"

Jeremiah stared down at them like they were so many juicy bugs waiting to be eaten by one hungry rooster!

People screamed and tires screeched. Cars skidded to a stop when their drivers saw the fifty-foot-tall Jeremiah standing on the road up ahead. One car slid out of control and . . .

K-BAMB!

... crashed into one of the farmers' booths. The booth toppled over, sending dozens of cantaloupes bouncing down the street like out-of-control bowling balls.

A woman cried, "YEOW!" as she tripped over one of the rolling fruits, reached out to keep her balance, and ...

K-RASH!

... pulled another booth to the ground, dumping 150 pounds of fresh yellow bananas onto the sidewalk. No problem. Well ... except for the folks running behind her who stepped on the ripe, soft fruit and ...

"OHHH ..."
"AHHH ..."
"EEEE ..."
"OOOO ..."

... went flying. Even that wasn't a problem until ...

SPLIT
SPLAT
SPLIF
SPLOP

... they landed facedown in the boxes of the various vegetables.

Yes, sir, Main Street was looking like a battlefield. People were falling and sprawling everywhere.

"I got it!" Melissa suddenly shouted. "I just figured out what's wrong with Jeremiah! He's hypnotized!"

"Hypnotized?" Sean cried.

"Yes! Somehow, he got hypnotized during the show. That's why he thinks he's a rooster!"

"But what's he doing up there?!" Sean shouted as he pointed to "Jeremiah the Humongous" towering over them.

"I don't know," Melissa yelled. "But maybe if we can bring him out of the trance . . ."

"How?"

"They said something, remember?" Melissa put her hands to her head, trying to recall what the hypnotists had said to bring their subjects out of their trances. "What was it . . . cookie? No, no. Donut? No, that's not it. *Something* sweet!" Suddenly she and Sean both remembered.

"Chocolate Cake!" they shouted to each other.

"DOO-A-DOODLE COCK!"

Jeremiah gave another mighty flap of his wings . . . er, arms.

Sean and Melissa looked up, cupping their hands to their mouths, and shouted as loud as they could.

"CHOCOLATE CAKE!"

49

Suddenly Jeremiah stopped flapping.

"CHOCOLATE CAKE!" they shouted again.

Now Jeremiah began looking around, obviously confused. "What . . . what . . . where?"

POOF!

Suddenly he was gone! Well, not gone, really, but back in Sean's digital watch, where he belonged.

"What happened?" he asked, shaking his little head.

"You were hypnotized!" Sean said. "You thought you were a rooster!"

"I did?" Jeremiah shook his head again. "Boy, do I feel like a clone."

I Haven't Been Myself Lately

MONDAY, 12:15 PDST

Melissa looked over the selections of the school cafeteria "food." *Maybe it would be better to skip lunch altogether*, she thought.

"Hon, you're holding up the line," the cafeteria lady said. She had a dirty apron and a big spoon. She pointed the spoon at a huge pan of something that looked suspiciously like pig slop. "So what will it be?" she asked. "The meatloaf or—" she tapped her spoon against a steaming tray of what looked like boiled cardboard— "Swiss steak?"

Melissa sighed. This was going to be a tough decision.

"Hon, people are waiting."

"Okay. Give me the pig slo—I mean, the meatloaf."

She watched as the woman spooned out a big helping of glop and plopped it onto her plate. Melissa could only shake her head. Mondays were bad enough without having to deal with cafeteria food.

Melissa picked up her tray and worked her way through the crowded room. She spotted Spalding over in the corner, sitting all alone. "Hey, Spalding," she called, "you were really hilarious Saturday."

"So I've been told," he said.

"Mind if I sit here?" she asked.

He shrugged. "Suit yourself."

Melissa plunked her lunch tray on the table and took a seat. Normally, she wouldn't go out of her way to speak to Spalding, but today was different. Today, she was working as a detective.

"Tell me," she said, "what was it like being hypnotized at the club Saturday?"

Spalding thought a moment. "I found it rather . . . refreshing."

Melissa nodded, then noticed Spalding didn't have a tray in front of him. "You on a diet or something?" she asked.

"Me? Certainly not." He gave one of his superior laughs—the one that says, *I'm so rich I don't know why I waste my time with such common riffraff*. "Actually," he continued, "I find it difficult to digest any of these culinary catastrophes. Instead, I find it far more appealing to bring my own nourishment." With that, he produced a small brown bag and pulled out a big handful of . . . KIBBLES 'N BITS!

"Dog food!" Melissa exclaimed. "You're eating dog food?"

"Certainly not," Spalding said in his snootiest voice. "It would be a grievous error to waste such delicious sustenance on mere dogs."

Melissa watched in disbelief as he stuffed the entire handful into his mouth. "Mmmmm . . ." he said, rolling his eyes as if he'd just tasted a delicious hot fudge sundae. "Delightful. Would you care for some?"

"Uh, no, thanks."

"Suit yourself," he said as he continued to crunch noisily. "All the more for me."

"Spalding . . . is this some kind of joke?" she asked. "Tell me you're not really eating Kibbles 'n Bits."

"I certainly am. I love it. Don't knock it if you haven't tried—"

K-BAMB!

Suddenly Spalding's two friends—KC, the toughest kid in town (even if she *is* a girl), and Bear, whose picture could be found in the dictionary under the word *lazy*— collided into each other. Normally, this wouldn't have been a problem, except they collided right behind Melissa. The good news was KC managed to hold on to her tray. The bad news was Bear did not, which meant . . .

K-SPLAT!

. . . pig slop . . . er, meatloaf . . . spilling all over Melissa.

Instantly, she jumped to her feet. "Oh, great!" she cried. "My brand-new top!"

"Sorry . . ." Bear sputtered. "It's just . . . when I saw Spalding there, eating dog food, I, uh, well that is to say . . ."

By now, Spalding had risen to his feet and offered to help. (Being a snob didn't mean he couldn't be a gentleman from time to time.) "Allow me," he said. "I have several tissues." He reached into his pocket, pulled out the "tissues," and began wiping the goo off Melissa.

Only they weren't tissues Spalding pulled out of his pocket. Instead, it was a fist full of twenty-dollar bills! Seeing the money, his mouth fell open in surprise. So did everyone else's. When he finally found his voice, all he could say was, "Where in the world did these come from? I only carry MasterCard!"

MONDAY, 13:12 PDST

Mrs. Applewhite turned back to the class. She had just written more mathematical equations on the blackboard than Sean had ever seen in his life.

"So," she said, dusting the chalk off her hands, "are there any questions?" She nodded to Spalding, who sat in the front with his hand raised. "Yes, Spalding?"

"Yes, Mrs. Applewhite. Would you please explain . . ."

But that was about all Sean understood of Spalding's question. The rest was spoken in "math-ese," that strange mathematical language full of Xs, Ys, and square roots. A language Sean was sure he'd never understand.

When he was done, Mrs. Applewhite nodded. "That's a very good question, Spalding."

It was? Sean wracked his brain trying to remember anything they'd studied that was even close to the question.

But Mrs. Applewhite understood perfectly. She turned back to the board. "You see," she began, scribbling furiously on the chalkboard, "when the coefficient of Y is two times pi . . ."

That was all it took. Upon saying the word, she suddenly stopped writing. It was almost as if she were frozen. Everyone waited, but she just stood there with her back to the class.

Finally, KC called out, "Mrs. Applewhite? Mrs. Applewhite . . . are you all right?"

Ever so slowly, she turned to face the class. "Of course," she said. "Why wouldn't I be all right?" She looked at the chalk in her hand. "But what am I doing with this?"

"Um . . ." KC cleared her throat. "You were just explaining what to do when the coefficient of Y is—"

"Coefficient of Y?" she said. "Heavens! That sounds like . . . like math or something."

"It *is* math," KC replied.

"Well," Mrs. Applewhite sniffed haughtily. "What would *I* possibly know about math?" She tossed the chalk back in its tray.

"But you're our teacher!" Bear answered.

"Teacher? You must be crazy! I'm not a teacher. I'm—" she twirled around—"a ballerina!"

Suddenly she began dancing around the room on her tiptoes. She kicked high in the air and—"Look out!"— the entire first row ducked for cover. She picked up some test papers and flung them into the air, dancing among them with her arms raised as they fluttered back to earth.

She whirled around clumsily, smashing into the class science project, which crashed to the floor. Then she careened into the bookcase, sending the entire set of Encyclopedia America cascading from their shelves.

"Bear!" Sean shouted. "Duck!"

Too late!

Mrs. Applewhite's next high kick caught Bear square on the nose.

But she didn't even notice. Instead, she kept on with her ballet (if that's what you call it). She took a flying leap toward her desk. Somehow, she actually made it to the top and began dancing on it. But amidst the laughter and giggles, Sean could hear a loud and clear . . .

CREEAK . . . GROAAN . . .

. . . which could only mean one thing: She was too heavy for the desk, and it was about to collapse.

He had to do something. But what?

GROAAN . . . CREEAK . . .

Wait a minute! Obviously, Mrs. Applewhite had gone back into the hypnotic trance she'd been in at the club. And, from what he remembered with Jeremiah, there was only one way out. He jumped to his feet and yelled, "Chocolate Cake!"

The other kids looked at him like he was crazy, but he didn't care. He tried again, louder. "Chocolate Cake!"

Suddenly Mrs. Applewhite stopped in midtwirl. "What? Where am I?" she asked.

"On top of your desk!" KC replied.

"Help! Somebody get me down!"

Several students rushed to her rescue. When she finally made it down, she stood shaking in front of her class. "I . . . I don't know what happened," she stuttered. "I was writing on the board, when suddenly . . ." She reached into her pocket for a handkerchief to dab the perspiration from her forehead.

There was a loud gasp from all the students.

"What's wrong?" she asked.

She glanced at the "handkerchief" she'd just pulled out. But it wasn't a handkerchief at all. Instead, it was a wad of twenty-dollar bills! Her eyes widened in surprise . . . and then she fainted.

MONDAY, 14:35 PDST

At the end of the day, Melissa joined Sean near the school parking lot to compare notes. "So, did you find any answers?" she asked.

Sean shook his head. "Just more questions."

"What do you mean?"

But before he could answer, they stopped in their tracks at the sight of a Midvale Police car in front of the school. A patrolman stood nearby. Sean and Melissa exchanged glances and then approached.

"Officer," Sean asked, "is everything all right?"

The policeman turned to them. "Not really," he answered. "Somebody broke into the school office earlier this morning. Got away with over three hundred dollars!"

5

Jesse James Strikes Again

MONDAY, 14:42 PDST

Sean kicked a pop can along in front of him as he and his sister slowly made their way from the school to Dad's station. "I can't believe the police didn't want our help," he complained.

"Me neither," Melissa agreed. "We keep solving cases for them, and they still don't want us around."

Sean sighed. "I guess we'll just have to solve this one for them, too . . . whether they like it or not." He stooped down, picked up the can, and using a neat over-the-shoulder hook shot, deposited it in a trash receptacle on the side of the street. "Swish!" he shouted. "Another three-pointer for Shaquille Hunter!"

Melissa shook her head. Boys . . . they could be so strange sometimes. One minute they're acting all grown-up—the next, they're shooting hook shots with pop cans. Weird.

"What I can't figure out," Sean said, "is how this all ties together."

"You really think there's a connection?" Melissa asked.

"There's gotta be. Look . . . Spalding gets up on stage at the comedy club and acts like a dog. The next thing we know, he's eating Kibbles 'n Bits for lunch. And then Mrs. Applewhite starts dancing Swan Lake right in the middle of math class. Not only that," he continued, "but Herbie says he's Jesse James and that both of them are members of his gang. Doesn't it seem strange to you that they both show up at school with big wads of money . . . and neither knows where it came from?"

"Look!" Melissa pointed. "Isn't that Herbie over there?"

About fifty yards up the street, a solitary figure walked toward them. It looked like Herbie, but it was hard to tell for sure since his hat was pulled down so far on his head that you couldn't see his eyes. And, even though it was a warm spring day, he had a heavy coat wrapped around him. Very strange.

But the closer he got, the more Melissa was sure it was him. Finally, she cried out, "Hi, Herbie!"

No answer.

"Herbie!" Sean called. "Where're you headed?"

Still nothing.

Melissa shot her brother a questioning look.

Sean answered, "He acts like he doesn't hear us."

By now he was within a few yards of them and there still wasn't the slightest trace of recognition. And then, as if that weren't odd enough, he walked right past them without so much as a word.

"What's going on?" Melissa whispered as they both turned to watch Herbie head down the street. "Where's he going?"

The two exchanged glances. Each knew there was only one way to find out.

MONDAY, 15:03 PDST

Twenty minutes later, Sean and Melissa found themselves standing across the street from Zomar the Magnificent's new counseling office, waiting for Herbie to come back out.

"I wonder what he's doing in there?" Melissa said.

"Beats me. But whatever it is—" Sean stopped in midsentence. "Here he comes."

Herbie emerged whistling happily to himself as he stepped into the bright sunlight.

"Notice anything strange?" Sean whispered.

"Yeah. He left his coat in there."

To the kids' surprise, Herbie looked over, smiled, and waved. "Hi, guys," he called out. "What's up?"

"We were about to ask you the same thing," Melissa answered.

"Me? Nothing. Just thought I'd go for a walk."

"So where's your coat?" Sean asked.

"Coat?" Herbie laughed. "Are you kidding? Why would I need a coat on a day like this?"

MONDAY, 15:29 PDST

Sean and Melissa watched through the glass of the control room as their Dad spoke into the microphone. "And next up, that romantic classic, 'Is It Love or Do I Just Need More Rolaids?' " He pressed a button on the CD player, and the music started. Then, pushing back his chair, he stood and stretched, turned down the mic, and walked out of the control room to join his children. "Hi, guys," he grinned.

"Hi, Dad." Melissa gave him a little hug.

"What brings you to the station?" he asked.

She threw Herbie a nervous glance. He was over by Katie, the elderly part-time receptionist, and doing what he did best: scarfing down leftover food.

"We were just wondering if everything is okay," Sean said.

"Sure. Why shouldn't it be?"

"No reason," Melissa said. "We just saw Herbie in town and decided to come by and say hello."

"Well," Dad grinned, "I'm glad you did. You guys up for some yogurt?"

Melissa motioned toward the empty control booth. "Aren't you on the air?"

"Herbie will cover for me . . . won't you, Herb?"

Glancing up with a mouthful of stale taco chips, Herbie sputtered, "No problem."

"Thanks. Come on, guys," Dad said, "let's go." They started out of the lobby when Dad stopped and turned back to Herbie. "Oh, we've got a commercial coming up for a new sponsor. It's written up and it's on the desk. Will you do it after the song?"

Herbie, who was busy washing down the stale chips with a half-empty can of even more stale soda, nodded.

"Thanks," Dad said. Then, turning to the receptionist, he asked, "Katie, I want to take the kids out for yogurt, but I'm a little short on cash. Think the station can float me a loan till payday?"

Katie pushed her glasses up her nose. "Well . . . seeing as how you own the station and everything, I guess it will be all right." She reached into the bottom drawer of her desk, pulled out an envelope, and suddenly cried, "Eeegh!"

"Katie! What is it?"

"The money!"

"What about it?"

"It's . . . gone!"

They all moved to the desk for a better look as the song wound down and Herbie entered the control booth to go on the air. Compared to his usual insecure self, when he spoke over the radio, Herbie always sounded smooth and sophisticated. "And now a word from Sergeant Mills Foods," he said. "Isn't it a relief to know that in this fast-paced world you can still fix your family a healthy, nutritious, well-balanced dinner? Why, with Sergeant Mills Foods, it's as easy as *pie*. . . ."

Suddenly Herbie's voice changed again. Only now he sounded like he was from some old Western. "And me and my gang," he shouted, "we're gonna have us all the gold in this here town before we're through!"

Everyone at Katie's desk turned and stared at Herbie. Dad frowned. "What on earth?"

"And nobody better try an' stop us, ya hear?"

"Oh no," Sean groaned. "He thinks he's Jesse James again."

Suddenly Herbie pointed his fingers as if they were guns and started blasting away at the microphone.

"BANG!" he shouted. "BANG! BANG! BANG!"

Melissa shook her head. She could just imagine what folks all over Midvale were thinking as they listened to this.

The good news was they didn't have to listen for long. Because Herbie had already risen and was running out of the control room. Once outside, he pointed his fingers directly into Dad's face and shouted, "Yeah . . . I took the money! I took it all! And if you try to stop me, I'll fill you so full of lead they'll use you for a number two pencil!"

He threw back his head, laughed, then ran out the door.

For a long moment, everyone stood in shock. Until, finally, Katie reached for the phone.

"Who are you calling?" Dad asked.

"We've just had $250 stolen," she said as she started to dial. "I think we should call the police, don't you?"

Slowly, sadly, Dad began to nod.

6

What's Up?

"Miffy, wegada dasumpn talperbie," Sean said.

Melissa looked at her brother. Since Dad had canceled the yogurt trip, Sean had talked her into stopping by Donut Delights to grab a little something to hold him over. A little something like three jelly donuts, two glazed donuts, a maple bar, and a carton of milk . . . most of which were in his mouth.

"What?" she said, not working too hard to cover her disgust.

He wiped his mouth, swallowed hard, and repeated. "I said, we've gotta do something to help Herbie." He crammed in another whole donut.

Melissa rolled her eyes. "Well, I'm happy to see that none of this has hurt your appetite."

"Hey . . . a guy's gotta eat!"

She watched in amazement as her brother finished the donut, gulped down the last half of the milk, and let out a long, loud . . . *BELCH*.

"Sorry." He flashed a sheepish grin.

She could only shake her head.

"Come on," he said, rising to his feet. "If we're going to crack this case, we can't sit around eating all day."

"Really?" Melissa asked, joining him. "I thought eating was your specialty."

Sean let the comment go as the two of them headed outside. They traveled several blocks and were just approaching their house when Melissa grabbed her brother's elbow. "Who in the world is that?"

"Where?"

"There," she pointed. Just ahead of them, someone of obviously great importance was walking in their direction. Better make that *two* someones of great importance. The first was dressed in flowing purple robes. On her head was a crown studded with jewels that sparkled in the sunlight.

"What's the queen of England doing in our neighborhood?" Melissa whispered.

"Queen?" Sean asked. "Looks more like somebody's fairy godmother!" He pointed toward the woman's left hand, where she held what looked like a magic wand.

"I think that's her royal scepter," Melissa whispered.

"And what in the world is that supposed to be?" Sean pointed at the creature walking ahead of her. It wore a gem-covered collar, a tiny purple coat all its own, and a miniature crown perched on its little head.

"That must be her royal cat!" Melissa exclaimed.

Sean and Melissa came to a stop and watched as Their Majesties slowly approached. You could tell by the way they walked that they were royalty. Those noses held high in the air. The way they puffed out their chests with pride. That haughty expression on Mrs. Tubbs' face.

Mrs. Tubbs?!

What on earth was Mrs. Tubbs doing dressed up like Queen Victoria? And Precious! The poor cat had never looked so ridiculous—well, except for the time Doc's invention Domesticus IV had accidentally shaved him from head to tail.

"Good afternoon, Mrs. Tubbs," Melissa said in her sweetest voice. She knew the woman didn't like them much. How could she when major catastrophes always seemed to happen whenever they were around?

"Harumph," Mrs. Tubbs answered.

"So, Mrs. Tubbs," Sean tried again. "You look very . . . um . . ."

"Nice!" Melissa interrupted before her brother said something stupid.

71

"*Nice* isn't exactly the word I was looking for," Sean said. "I was thinking more like *weir*—"

Melissa gave him a sharp poke in the ribs. "Like *we're* really wondering where you got such beautiful clothes," she said.

"That's right," her brother agreed, trying to avoid another painful blow. "Are you on your way to a costume party or something?"

"I most certainly am not!" Mrs. Tubbs raised her nose a notch higher into the air.

"Sorry," Sean said. "We've just never seen you dressed like this before. So, naturally, we were wondering . . ."

"Well, if you must know," Mrs. Tubbs answered, "Precious and I went to see those two wonderful men at their new therapy office downtown."

"Zomar the Magnificent?" Sean asked.

"And Larry?" Melissa added.

"That's right. They took me through some marvelous past-life regression."

"You too?" Melissa asked.

"Certainly. As you know, we have all lived many lives before this one. But we can only remember them with the help of hypnosis."

"Mrs. Tubbs," Sean began, "you don't really believe that, do you?"

"And why wouldn't I?" she asked.

From past cases, Sean knew the answer and didn't hesitate to give it. "Well, the Bible says we only die once . . . and after that we go stand before God in judgment."

"Well, obviously," she said, adjusting her crown, "the Bible is wrong."

Sean and Melissa exchanged glances.

"So . . ." Melissa ventured, "the reason you're dressed this way is because it has something to do with a past life you think you lived?"

"Not just one life!" Mrs. Tubbs snapped, standing as tall and straight as she could. "Several lives! It seems that I have been a long line of royal women."

"Pardon me?" Melissa asked. The poor lady was sounding crazier by the minute.

"Not only was I Queen Victoria, but I was also Queen Elizabeth the First! And before that I was Cleopatra. And before that, Helen of Troy!"

"But I thought Helen of Troy was a fictional charact—" Another poke in the ribs cut Sean short in midsentence.

Mrs. Tubbs continued. "So, naturally, when I discovered all of that, I wanted to dress appropriately!" She gestured toward her snooty cat. "And Precious here . . . did you know that he was actually Napoleon?"

"You mean he was Napoleon's cat?" Sean asked.

"No, you silly boy! He *was* Napoleon!"

"Meooow!" said Precious, sounding very full of himself.

"Woof! Woof!"

Sean and Melissa turned to their house to see Slobs leaping against the backyard fence. If there was one sound Slobs disliked, it was Precious's prideful meowing.

"Slobs, no!" Sean shouted.

But knowing full well how to bother the dog, Precious howled all the louder. "Meooow!"

The dog began jumping at the fence. "Woof! Woof!"

"Slobs!" Melissa shouted.

And then louder some more. "MEOOOW!"

"WOOF! WOOF!"

"Slobs?!"

But that was all the dog could take. After several leaps against the wire fence, he had finally pushed it down enough to leap over it. With one giant jump, Slobs was over the fence and racing toward them.

"Slobs! No!"

"Keep that nasty dog away from my—"

"MEOWRR! HISSSSS!"

"WOOF! WOOF!"

And the chase began. . . .

Precious took off, while Slobs bounded after him in delight. The only problem was that Mrs. Tubbs was once again hanging on to the leash. (Some people never learn.)

"Mrs. Tubbs, let go of the leash! MRS. TUBBS!"

But the poor lady didn't hear. She was too busy . . .

"AUGH!"

. . . screaming for her life!

The cheetah may be the fastest animal on earth, but it would have eaten dust trying to keep up with Precious as he raced ahead of Slobs.

"Slobs! Stop!" Sean and Melissa ran after them as fast as they could, but it was no use. As usual, the leash was so wrapped around Mrs. Tubbs' hand that she couldn't let go even if she wanted to. And boy, did she want to!

Remember Billy Williams' skateboard? Well, the good news was Billy had put it away. The bad news was he had a little sister, Becky Williams . . . who had a little red wagon . . . who had not put it away. So, sure enough . . .

K-THUNK

. . . Mrs. Tubbs tripped over it, went flying through the air, and . . .

K-PLOP

. . . did her standard belly flop directly into it.

"Help me!" she screamed as she rolled down the sidewalk. Her head was just inches from the ground as her purple robe flew in every direction. "HELP!"

75

Unfortunately, it was at this exact time that Mr. Miller, the neighborhood postman, was making his rounds. And, even more unfortunately, the poor fellow wasn't so good in the hearing department. In fact, Precious, Mrs. Tubbs, and the wagon were nearly on top of him before he turned around and . . .

"LOOK OUT!" Mrs. Tubbs screamed.

The good news was the man was able to leap out of their way just in time as cat, woman, and wagon zipped by. The bad news was he wasn't so lucky with Slobs.

"WOOF! WOO—"

K-BLAM!

Slobs ran into him, sending both the man and his bag of letters high into the air.

"Mr. Miller, Mr. Miller," Melissa cried, running to him. "Are you all right?"

The poor man nodded but definitely looked dazed as hundreds of letters that had flown into the air were now raining down upon them.

Meanwhile, Mrs. Tubbs continued her race down the sidewalk with her head so close to the ground that the points of her crown began picking up souvenirs along the way.

THWACK!

An empty milk carton here.

THUNK!

A half-eaten apple there.

SSSHHHKKK!

A wadded-up fast-food bag. Then, with the last remaining spike of her crown . . .

KER-SPLAT!

. . . a rotten orange.

She continued past a city work crew picking up litter along the road. As she flashed by with the fresh load of garbage on her head, one man turned to the other and said, "I hope they don't expect us to do that."

The other fellow scratched his head and replied, "I don't know . . . looks like a pretty effective way of picking up garbage to me."

At last the wagon hit a curb and . . .

K-THUNK!
"AUGH!"

. . . Mrs. Tubbs was thrown out of the wagon. She managed to stagger to her feet. Unfortunately, she still hadn't managed to let go of the leash.

Too bad, because the Midvale Community College lay

just ahead. No problem, except that Precious took a left turn and headed straight for the athletic field. Even that wouldn't have been so bad if the all-district track meet hadn't just begun.

K-BLEWY!

The official fired his pistol to begin the 440 race. Just as the athletes pushed off their blocks, running as fast as they could go, Precious pulled onto the track behind them.

The runners raced forward, but they were no match for the frightened cat. Still pulling Mrs. Tubbs behind him, Precious caught up to the last-place runner on the first turn.

The roar from the crowd grew deafening as thousands of people in the stands jumped to their feet in excitement.

The race continued. Mrs. Tubbs moved to fifth place . . . then fourth . . . then third . . . then second!

Now she was gaining on the leader!

The crowd went wild! People were yelling! Screaming! Waving their programs in excitement!

At last, Mrs. Tubbs pulled alongside the leader.

Poor guy. He was straining and stretching with everything he had. But all it took was one set of barks from Slobs . . .

"WOOF! WOOF!"

and . . .

BYE! BYE!

Precious zoomed forward, leaving the guy far behind. In fact, all three of them—Precious, Mrs. Tubbs, and Slobs—crossed the finish line a good twenty paces ahead of him.

The judge held out a blue ribbon, but Mrs. Tubbs just kept on going, heading straight for . . .

"OH NO!" she screamed. "NOT THE HURDLES!"

"Oh yes!"

THUNK! . . . "OW!" . . . THUNK! . . . "OW!" . . . THUNK! . . . "OW!"

The cat was jumping over the hurdles just fine. But poor Mrs. Tubbs was crashing into every one of them.

"BOO! HISS!"

The very crowd that had been cheering her on just a few moments earlier was now jeering at her. But it made no difference to Precious. He'd had enough sports for one day. He took a hard right, raced across the field, and ran back toward the street.

But Slobs, who had been following, suddenly came to a screeching halt. Precious and Mrs. Tubbs continued racing out of sight, but the bloodhound no longer followed. As far as she was concerned, the chase was over. Something else had caught her attention.

It took Sean and Melissa several moments before they finally caught up to her . . . wheezing and gasping all the way.

"What (*wheeze, wheeze*) is it, girl?" Sean asked.

Slobs wagged her tail and whined.

"What's (*gasp, gasp*) wrong?" Melissa asked.

More whining and tail wagging until the brother and sister followed the dog's gaze up to the top branch of a nearby tree. Something was indeed up. And it was . . . Herbie! He clung to the tiny branch, shaking in fear.

"Herbie?" Sean approached the tree. "Herbie, what are you doing up there?"

Melissa joined her brother's side. "Herbie, are you all right?"

"You've gotta help me!" he cried.

"What is it?" Sean asked. "What's going on?"

"The police are after me!" he said. "They tried to arrest me, and I don't know why! I haven't done anything."

Sean and Melissa exchanged skeptical looks.

"Please!" he cried. "You've got to help me. You've got to help!"

7

Something's Burning

MONDAY, 16:45 PDST

Chief Robertson broke out laughing. "How can you two say Herbie is innocent? His fingerprints were all over the empty cash envelope at the radio station."

Sean and Melissa traded looks. It had taken a while, but they had finally convinced Herbie to come down out of the tree and turn himself in to the police. They were positive that it was all a big mix-up and that as soon as things got straightened out everything would be okay. No way was Herbie a criminal.

Unfortunately, their friend Chief Robertson wasn't buying it. "We also found his fingerprints in a few other interesting places," he said.

"Like where?" Sean asked.

"Like the cash register at the comedy club. And inside the school office."

"The school office?" Melissa asked.

The chief nodded. "Yup. The janitor said he saw a fellow matching your buddy's description hanging around outside the school right after it was broken into. And later he was seen giving wads of what looked like money to your friend Spalding and also to Mrs. Applewhite."

"You think he gave them some of the stolen money?" Sean asked. "But why?"

"Remember how at the comedy club he called them his brother and sister?" Chief asked.

Both kids nodded.

"The way we figure it, he must have thought he was looking out for them."

"This is crazy, Chief," Sean said. "Maybe Herbie took the money, I don't know. But if he did, it was only because he's under some kind of spell or something."

"Spell?" the chief asked.

Melissa nodded. "We figure this has something to do with those hypnotist guys," Melissa said.

"Larry and Zomar?" the chief asked. "You've gotta be kidding. Those guys are great! I've been to them for therapy myself, and they really helped. As a matter of fact, I've asked all my officers to set up therapy appointments . . . you know, to help them deal with the everyday stress they face on the job."

"But . . . but . . ." Sean sputtered, "Herbie's innocent!"

Suddenly there was a loud knock on the chief's door. "Come in."

The door opened, and a uniformed officer poked his head in. "We got him," he grinned. "This Herbie guy has finally confessed."

"To which crime?" Chief asked.

"To all of them."

Herbie sat on a small cot inside his dimly lit cell. He looked sad and scared. When he spotted Sean and Melissa approaching, his face brightened, but only slightly. "Hi, guys," he sighed as he got up and walked over to the iron bars separating them.

"Are you all right?" Melissa asked.

He shrugged. "Looks like I'm in a bit of trouble."

"They say you confessed to robbing the radio station," Sean said.

"And the school," Melissa added.

"Yeah." Herbie took another deep breath and sighed. "I don't remember, but I must have done it. I mean, I had the station's money right on me. And my fingerprints were all over the school."

"But if you don't remember, why did you confess?" Melissa asked.

"Let's face it, kids," Herbie sighed, "I'm just a bad guy. It's in my nature."

"What are you talking about?" Sean said. The very thought of Herbie as a criminal was ridiculous. This was a man who wouldn't even make a right turn on a red light. He spent Tuesday nights reading stories to the kids at the Midvale Children's Home, and every Sunday afternoon found him visiting his mother at the Shady Grove Nursing Home. Not exactly the sort of things "bad guys" do.

"Well, you know," Herbie said, "I *was* Jesse James in a past life. I guess I can't help myself. I see somebody else's money, and I just naturally—"

"That's ridiculous!" Sean interrupted.

"It sure is!" Melissa added. "You're not a criminal . . . and we're gonna get you out of here!"

Herbie turned away and walked back to his cot. "Don't bother," he sighed as he sat down. "I'm being punished for what I did wrong. Right here is where I need to stay."

MONDAY, 17:30 PDST

Sean and Melissa headed home in silence, trying to figure out their next step.

"What's down, duds?"

Sean glanced down at his watch and saw Jeremiah smiling up at him, his skin emitting a healthy green glow.

"What do mean, *duds?*" Sean asked.

"I think he means *dudes*," Melissa said. "As in, *'What's up, dudes?'*"

Jeremiah shrugged and continued, "I have news from Doc."

"What is it?" Melissa asked.

"Uh . . ." Jeremiah scratched his head, sending sparks flying from his bright red hair. "Something about . . . something."

"She knows something about the case?" Sean asked hopefully.

"No . . . it's more like . . . uh . . ."

"The thinking cap?" Melissa asked. "Did she get the thinking cap fixed?"

"That's it! You hit the nail right on the sliver lining! She's made some modifications, and she wants you to come over tomorrow to help her try it out!"

Sean nodded. "Tell her we'll be over right after schoo—"

"So . . . talking to your imaginary friend again?"

Sean and Melissa looked up to see their not-so-great pals KC and Bear, who had just come around the corner. At the sound of KC's voice, Jeremiah quickly disappeared from Sean's watch, leaving him to fend for himself.

"No . . . no . . . I was just . . . uh . . ."

Melissa came to his rescue by changing the subject. "And just who are you guys supposed to be?" She was referring to the brown leather jacket and old-fashioned aviator goggles KC was wearing . . . and the Davy Crockett–style coonskin cap on Bear's head.

"Who am I *supposed* to be?" KC scorned. "You mean, who *am* I?" she corrected.

"She's Amelia Earhart," Bear explained.

"What are you talking about?" Sean asked.

"We went in and had a past-life reading," KC said. "And I found out that in a former life, I was the famous aviator Amelia Earhart!"

"Oh no," Sean muttered underneath his breath. "Here we go again."

"And Bear here . . . Well, why don't you tell them who you were!"

Bear thought hard for a minute. "I don't remember. Who was I again?"

"Daniel Boone!" KC answered in frustration. "You were Daniel Boone!"

"Yeah. That's right. I was Daniel Boone."

"You don't really believe that stuff, do you?" Melissa asked.

"And why shouldn't we?" KC demanded.

Sean shrugged. "It's just that the Bible says we only die once . . . and after that we stand in front of God to be judged. It doesn't say anything about second chances or coming back over and over again."

"Well . . . maybe the Bible's wrong," Bear said.

Melissa answered, "If I have to choose between what the Bible says and what those hypnotists are saying, I gotta tell you, I'd choose the Bible every time."

KC shrugged. "You can believe that old-fashioned stuff if you want," she said with a haughty voice. "But I always knew I had greatness in me. Come on, Bear, let's go."

With that, the two headed off down the street.

"Well, what do you think of that?" Sean asked as they watched them go.

Melissa slowly shook her head. "Not much," she said. "Not much at all."

TUESDAY, 14:48 PDST

The following day after school, they arrived at Doc's and climbed the rickety old stairs up to her attic laboratory. After greeting them, the scientist proudly led them to a workbench where the new and improved thinking cap sat. It was much smaller. The huge tubes were gone and replaced by tiny computer chips.

Sean picked it up and placed it carefully on his head, but now it was so small it didn't even fit.

"Uh-oh," Melissa said, "too small."

"Don't be ignorant," Sean answered. "It just needs . . ." He grabbed the edges of the cap and began yanking it down hard on top of his head. ". . . a little . . ." Over and over again he pulled until he finally squeezed inside it. ". . . help, that's all." Once it was on his head, he turned to his sister. "Okay, now give me some juice."

"Sean," Melissa warned, "I don't think that's such a smart—"

"Will you stop worrying! Just crank this puppy up."

Melissa sighed wearily. Sean obviously learned nothing from his previous experience. She nodded to Doc, who pushed a tiny button on the side of his cap.

"Feel anything?" Melissa asked.

"Not yet. Maybe you'd better turn it up a little—wait

a minute. Yes! Something's happening!" He snapped his fingers. "I see it! I see it! E really does equal MC squared! It's all becoming clear!"

He started pacing back and forth across the room. "I can't believe I never saw this before!"

"Okay, Sean!" Melissa cried. "That's enough! Turn it off! Turn it off this second!"

"Why should I?"

"Because your head is smoking!"

8

The Plan

TUESDAY, 15:08 PDST

"Sean!" Melissa screamed again. "Turn it off!"

Sean reached up for the control knob on the side of the cap.

It was stuck!

He twisted it harder, as hard as he could . . . but it still wouldn't move.

"What'll I do now?" he cried.

"Take it off!" his sister shouted.

Sean yanked at the helmet, but it wouldn't budge.

"I can't!" he shouted. "It's stuck!"

"I knew this would happen!" Melissa cried. "I just knew it!"

But Sean was in no mood to listen to his sister's lecture. Instead, he ran in tight little circles around the room as thick black smoke billowed out from underneath the stuck cap.

"Maybe you're thinking too hard!" Melissa shouted. "Try to stop thinking!" (She figured that wouldn't be too hard, at least for Sean.)

"I can't!" Sean wailed. "My brain is going a thousand miles an hour, and it won't quit!"

Doc grabbed a fire extinguisher from under her workbench and took aim at Sean's head. Melissa leaned back and prepared for the onslaught of foam. But when Doc pressed the handle, nothing happened—just a few drops of liquid that dribbled out of the nozzle and fell to the floor.

Doc shook the fire extinguisher and tried again. Nothing.

"DO SOMETHING!" Sean cried. "This thing is getting HOT!"

Doc threw the fire extinguisher to the ground and grabbed one side of the cap. Melissa grabbed the other. Together they pulled as hard as they could, but it wouldn't move. They tried again.

"OW!" Sean cried. "You're pulling my head off!"

The smoke grew thicker.

Suddenly Melissa noticed big tears rolling down Sean's cheeks. She seldom saw him cry, but whenever she did, it broke her heart.

"Don't cry," she pleaded. "We'll get you out of there!"

"I'm not crying!" he lied. "I'm . . . I'm . . . My eyes are just sweating, that's all!"

Jeremiah appeared on Doc's computer monitor. He was wearing Bermuda shorts, a tank top, and was cooling himself with a hand-held electric fan. "Is it just me," he shouted, "or is it getting hot in here?"

"Help us!" Melissa shouted. "Sean's head is smoking!"

"Uh-oh!" The color quickly drained from Jeremiah's face, leaving him looking like an old-fashioned black-and-white cartoon.

"You got any suggestions?" Melissa cried.

"Well, you know what they always say. . . ."

"What?"

"Where there's smoke, there's pliers."

"Pliers?" she cried. "What's that supposed to—"
Suddenly a light went on in Melissa's head. Without a word, she raced to Doc's tool chest and rummaged around until she pulled out a pair of pliers. She ran back to Sean and used them to take hold of the control knob of his cap. Once she got a good grip on the knob, she used all of her strength to try to twist it. The heat of the helmet made it hard, but at last she managed to twist the knob to the OFF position.

One last puff of smoke rose from Sean's head. And then there was nothing.

Relieved, Sean sank to the floor in the corner of the room, holding his head in his hands.

"Are you okay?" Melissa asked.

"Yeah . . . I think so," he half whispered. "Thanks . . ."

She nodded. "Thank Jeremiah. It was his idea."

"Don't mention it," the little guy quipped from a nearby monitor. Now that the crisis had passed, he was back to his full, glorious, Technicolor self. "I'm just glad I could help. After all, a friend in need is worth two in the bush."

Melissa reached down and patted her brother on top of the helmet. It slid off his head and crashed to the floor.

They stared at it in surprise.

"How'd you do that?" he asked.

"I don't know. It just . . . came off."

Sean shook his head. "Maybe all that heat expanded the metal."

Melissa nodded. "That was close," she said.

"All's well that ends without someone's hair being burned off," Jeremiah offered.

Suddenly concerned, Sean reached up and felt the top of his head. Good. His hair was still there. At least he thought so. "Do I look okay?" he asked. "My hair's not burnt, is it?"

"You look fine," Melissa said.

Not entirely convinced, Sean rose and crossed to a nearby mirror to check out his reflection. "Yeah," he nodded while looking at himself. "You're right. I'm just as gorgeous as ever." With that, he reached into his pocket, pulled out his comb, and began primping away.

Good grief, Melissa thought, *and he thinks I'm vain.* Unfortunately, just then he combed a clump of hair to the side, revealing a HUGE bald spot. Apparently, the heat of the cap singed the hair right off in that spot.

Melissa threw a nervous glance to Doc, who saw it, too. Doc turned back to her. Each knew what the other was thinking:

Should we tell him?

Melissa looked back at the bald spot. It reminded her of one of those monks with the whole middle part of their head shaved. Finally she turned back to Doc and shook her head. No, they wouldn't tell him. He'd find out soon enough on his own.

TUESDAY, 15:45 PDST

While Doc set about making some more adjustments to the thinking cap, Sean and Melissa began another one of their discussions about the comedy club mystery. It had become more than "just another case." Now Herbie was in trouble, and that made it personal.

Maybe he had stolen the money, but they knew he wouldn't have done it if he was in his "right" mind. No, something else was going on, and poor Herbie was getting blamed for it.

"It's got to involve those hypnotist guys," Sean insisted. "I mean, that's when things started to get weird."

Melissa nodded. "But how?"

Sean shook his head.

"And even if it did involve them, who could we get to believe us?"

"Obviously not the police," Sean said. "You heard Chief Robertson—he loves those guys."

"And everyone's sure they've already got their man," Melissa added.

"Everyone, including Herbie."

Melissa nodded. "Everyone but us."

"Uh, guys?" It was Jeremiah again. This time he was speaking from Sean's watch. "Listen, I don't mean to be a bother, but—"

"What's up?" Sean asked.

"There's a news report coming on over channel seven you need to see."

Sean and Melissa exchanged looks, then quickly rose and headed over to one of Doc's TVs.

A reporter with a microphone in hand filled the screen. Behind her, other news and TV reporters were jockeying for position.

"This is Bobbie Waters for Earwitness News. I'm standing outside the Midvale Courthouse, where a startling confession moments ago brought an end to a crime wave that has long tormented the citizens of Midvale."

Suddenly the screen was filled with a photograph of Herbie. He wore prison-issue denims and held a jail identification card in front of him.

"Herbie!" both kids cried out.

Bobbie Waters continued. "In an appearance before Judge Morton T. Burton, Herbie Olsen has now confessed to a dozen other unsolved crimes. Burton, who is known in Midvale as 'the Hanging Judge,' has scheduled sentencing of Mr. Olsen for the following Monday."

"I can't believe it!" Melissa cried.

"And finally," the reporter concluded just a little too dramatically, "the good citizens of Midvale—and the rest of the county—can sleep securely knowing that a dangerous criminal has finally been removed from our midst. This is Bobbie Waters for Earwitness News . . . where you always hear it first."

Sean looked at Melissa. Melissa looked at Sean. "What are we going to do?" she groaned.

But Sean was already thinking. "Hang on," he said, trying to piece things together. "Just give me a second." He began to pace.

"What?" Melissa asked.

He turned to look back at the thinking cap Doc was working on.

"What?" Melissa repeated.

Finally, he answered, "We both believe the key lies with those hypnotist guys, right?"

"Right."

"I mean, they're the ones who got Herbie into thinking he was Jesse James in the first place, right?"

"Right."

"So the solution is to get into their offices and see how they're doing what they're doing."

"But how?" Melissa demanded.

Sean broke into a small smile that grew bigger as he looked over to the thinking cap. "Not to worry, little sister," he said with a knowing chuckle. "Your brilliant big brother has a plan."

"Oh no," Melissa moaned. "As if we don't have enough problems already."

9

The Spell

TUESDAY, 15:58 PDST

As Doc worked on the thinking cap, Sean moved to where she could see his lips and asked, "Did you find the problem?"

She reached over and typed on the keyboard:

Just a minor miscalculation. I've decided to switch the operation of the unit to remote control. Much safer that way.

"Could this increase someone's brain power to the point that they couldn't be hypnotized?" he asked.

Doc quickly typed:

Absolutely.

"How long would it take to make two of these caps?" Sean asked.

About a day. Once the prototype is finished, the rest is easy.

"Sean," Melissa said uneasily, "I'm not sure what you're getting at, but there's no way I'm putting my head into one of those things."

"Come on, sis," he said. "It didn't hurt me any!" He stooped down to take a closer look at the cap, which brought his huge bald spot into her view.

Melissa wanted to answer, but all she could do was stare at the back of his head.

WEDNESDAY, 16:20 PDST

The following day, Mrs. Tubbs sat in the hypnotherapy office, holding her hand to her collar in mock surprise. "Really?" she asked. "I was really Marie Antoinette?"

"Yes, you were, Mrs. Tubbs." Larry smiled as he gently took her hand in his. "And Madame Curie!"

"Well, I certainly am glad I came back for another session."

"So am I, Mrs. Tubbs," Larry said as he patted her hand. "It's a rare privilege to be in the presence of such a distinguished and . . . uh . . ."

"Noble?" Mrs. Tubbs offered.

"Yes . . . that's the word I was looking for. Such a distinguished and noble soul."

Mrs. Tubbs turned her eyes toward the floor, trying her best to look humble . . . though, of course, it was impossible to pull it off.

Larry looked at his watch and stood. "I'm sorry, Mrs. Tubbs. I wish we could go on, but it looks like it's time for my next appointment."

She rose to her feet and extended her hand. "Well, thank you. It's been very enlightening."

Larry took her hand in both of his. "It's my pleasure, Mrs. Tubbs. You have lived hundreds of times—and each life has been more wonderful than the last!"

"Oh, my goodness! I'll have to come back again so you can tell me more."

"You do that, Mrs. Tubbs," he smiled. "You come back anytime." He lightly kissed the back of her hand.

Mrs. Tubbs blushed slightly, then practically floated out of the room.

As she closed the door to the office behind her, Zomar the Magnificent entered from the back room. "How'd it go?" he asked.

Larry shook his head. "People in this town will believe *anything*! Especially *that* one."

Zomar laughed. "It's incredible how they keep falling for this past-lives stuff, isn't it?"

"They're idiots!" Larry sneered. "They deserve everything that's about to happen to them . . . and to their stupid little town."

Zomar nodded. "I'll be so glad when it's over and we can get out of here. I hate this place!"

"Very soon, my friend. Very soon."

WEDNESDAY, 16:50 PDST

A half hour later, Melissa sat in the waiting room of the hypnotherapy office and giggled.

"What's wrong?" Sean asked.

"With all these bandages on our heads, it makes us look like mummies or something."

"Well, at least mine are on straight," Sean said. He knew that would get her. And sure enough, it did. Suddenly she started fiddling with her own bandages, making sure every one was in its proper place. *Girls*, he thought, *do they ever stop caring about their looks?*

The bandages had been Sean's idea. They were the only way to hide the thinking caps. The very thinking caps that would hopefully stop them from being hypnotized.

Suddenly the door to the waiting room opened and Larry came through wearing a dazzling smile.

"Good afternoon and welcome to . . . oh, my goodness, what happened to you two?"

"We were in an accident," Sean said.

"Yes, I can see that!" Larry clucked sympathetically as he motioned them into his office. "It must have been terrible. What happened?"

"Well," Melissa started, "we fell off of a, um—"

"Horse," Sean interrupted. Which, unfortunately, was the same time Melissa came up with "bicycle."

Larry looked confused. "I'm afraid I don't understand how—"

"It was like this," Sean said. "We were trying to ride a horse . . ."

" . . . *and* a bicycle," Melissa added.

"At the same time!" Sean said.

Melissa threw him an exasperated look. What *was* he saying now?

Realizing he might have gone too far, Sean tried to cover. "You know . . . to, uh, to get our names in the *Guiness Book of Records.*"

"I see."

"Well, I can tell you," Sean continued, "it's not as easy as you may think."

"I bet."

"Especially backward."

Melissa shot him another look

"Backward?" Larry asked.

"That's right," Sean added, getting caught up in his own story. "Everything was going okay until Misty here fell off . . ."

"I see."

" . . . and the horse stepped on her head."

"Ouch!" Larry said.

"And then . . . and then . . ." Running out of steam, Sean finally turned to his sister for help.

"And then my bike flew out of control and ran over you?" she offered.

"Yeah," Sean agreed. "Yeah, that's it!" He could feel perspiration gathering under his bandages. He wished they'd rehearsed the story before they came. And he hoped all of this sweating wouldn't cause an electrical short in his cap.

"Tell me," Larry asked suspiciously, "does the *Guiness Book of Records* really have a category for riding a horse and a bike at the same time?"

Realizing he might get caught, Sean suddenly replied, "No. That's the worst part. We did it all for nothing."

"Uh-huh," Larry nodded. "Er . . . would you kids please excuse me for a moment? I have to check on something. I'll be right back."

Larry found Zomar sitting behind his desk eating a bologna sandwich. "Hey," he whispered, "you'll find this hard to believe, but I've got a couple kids in the office right now who make Mrs. Tubbs seem like Albert Einstein."

Zomar suddenly stopped eating. "So you think maybe. . . ?"

Larry nodded. "Yes, I do. We can pin all the blame on them. By the time the cops figure out who really did it, we'll be out of the state!"

Meanwhile, Doc sat in her laboratory, staring at glowing red lights on a control panel. These indicated the condition of the two thinking caps on the kids' heads over a mile away. So far, everything was working perfectly. The power was strong, and it didn't look like either Sean or Melissa was in any danger. Just the same, she'd feel a lot better when this was over and the kids came back to the lab.

Wait a minute? Was it her imagination or was one of the lights becoming dimmer? She moved in for a better look.

Oh no! The power to Sean's cap! It was growing weaker! Frantically, she began adjusting the power until one of the lights suddenly began to flash off and on. Desperately, she checked and double-checked the controls until she finally found the reason. It was just as she feared. . . .

Sean's cap was shorting out!

By now, Larry had returned to the examination room and Sean was asking a question. "We understand that you can hypnotize people and take them into what they think are their past lives."

"That's right."

"Well, we'd like to find out who we were . . . you know . . . before we were us."

"Excellent," Larry grinned. He pulled a sparkling crystal on a chain out of his desk drawer and dangled it in front of them.

"Keep your eyes on the crystal," he said in a soothing voice. "Focus. Focus. You can't turn your eyes away. Your eyes are growing heavy . . . very, very heavy. . . ."

Melissa had to admit, the guy was good. In fact, even with the thinking cap, it took all of her concentration not to give in.

"I'm going to count backward from ten to one," Larry droned. "When I reach one, you will be completely asleep."

Sean and Melissa stared straight ahead.

"Ten . . . nine . . . eight . . . You're growing sleepy. Seven . . . six . . . five . . ."

Melissa had to concentrate even harder.

"You can no longer stay awake. Five . . . four . . . three . . . two . . . one . . ."

When he reached "one," Melissa closed her eyes and pretended to be asleep. She figured Sean was doing the same thing . . . though she thought his snoring was a bit overdramatic.

"Now," Larry continued, "I'm going to say a very special word that is going to put you into an even deeper trance. That word is *pie*. When I say *pie*, you will lose all power to resist me. You will do everything I say. Do you understand?"

Melissa nodded her head.

Larry smiled with satisfaction. "Pie!"

Melissa continued to sit with her head bowed and eyes closed.

Larry's grin grew bigger. He turned to Sean. "Now, young man, tell me again why you've come here today."

"We . . . came . . . here . . . because . . . we . . . wanted

... to ... find ... out ... what ... you ... are ... really ... up ... to."

What's he doing? Melissa thought with alarm. *He's telling him our plan! What is he thinking? Is he trying to ruin our chances? Or*—a cold thought ran through her mind—*or is he really hypnotized?* She tried not to show the fear growing inside of her. But she was definitely worried. Big time. *Please, God*, she silently prayed. *What do we do now?!*

"And what makes you think we're up to something?" Larry asked her sleeping brother.

"Because ... of ... all ... the ... robberies ... in ... town."

"I see. And you, young lady? Did you really think you could come here and not be hypnotized?"

Melissa swallowed hard, trying to come up with an answer. But she didn't need to.

"We ... are ... wearing ... thinking ... caps ... to ... keep ... us ... from ... being ... hypnotized," Sean said.

Melissa's heart sank.

"Thinking caps?" Larry threw back his head and laughed. "That's the dumbest thing I've ever heard."

Doc worked feverishly, trying to restore power to Sean's cap. But it was no use. The light on the control panel blinked once . . . twice . . . and then not at all.

There was nothing more she could do.

Sean and Melissa remained sitting with their heads bowed and their eyes closed.

"Repeat after me," Larry commanded. "Larry and Zomar are not up to anything."

"Larry . . . and . . . Zomar . . . are . . . not . . . up . . . to . . . anything," the young detectives repeated. Sean because he was under the spell. Melissa because she was pretending to be.

"They are two great and wonderful men."

"They . . . are . . . two . . . great . . . and . . . wonderful . . . men."

"Now, in a few moments," Larry explained, "I am going to bring you both out of your trances by saying the words *chocolate cake*. But even though you will be completely awake and alert in every way, you will still be under my spell. Is that understood?"

Sean and Melissa both nodded.

"I have a little something I want you to do for me," Larry laughed. "Tonight, at 10:00, you two are going to be robbing the Midvale National Bank!"

10

Cracking the Case

WEDNESDAY, 17:05 PDST

Sean shook his head. They had just left the hypnotists' office, and now as they headed home, he and Melissa were fighting. "What are you talking about?" he scorned. "Larry and Zomar aren't bad guys. In fact, they're *great and wonderful men*."

"No," Melissa argued. "That's what they hypnotized you to believe. They're really crooks!"

"They didn't hypnotize me," Sean insisted. "I was wearing the thinking cap!"

"It must not have been working!"

Sean started to answer, but it was getting hard to piece it all together. As a matter of fact, at the moment, he was having the world's worst headache.

"Sean," she insisted, "think about it! Why else would

they tell us to come to Midvale National Bank at 10:00 P.M. and bring trash bags?"

"I don't remember anything about that," he said while rubbing his head. "Listen, do you have any aspirin or something?"

Melissa reached into her handbag and began fishing around. Sean watched in amazement as she pulled out one comb, two brushes, two sticks of lip gloss, mascara, one can of hair spray, one bottle of antibacterial soap, two textbooks, three types of fingernail polish, one wallet, an address book, three cassette tapes, sixty-seven cents in loose change, a pocket-size Bible, and, oh yes . . . a small bottle of aspirin.

"Boy, sis," he said as he gratefully accepted the aspirin, "don't ever get mad and hit somebody with that bag. You'd probably kill 'em!"

WEDNESDAY, 21:45 PDST

"Sean . . . are you in there?" Melissa banged hard on his bedroom door, but there was no response.

She glanced at the hall clock. It was getting late.

"Sean . . . come on! Open up!"

Her brother wasn't crazy about her barging into his room without an invitation, but this was important, so she threw open the door and looked inside. It was the usual national disaster area. But worse than that was the fact that he was already gone! She was too late! She spun around and raced toward the hall steps. Not, of course, without stopping at the mirror to make sure her hair was okay. After all, there was no reason to go out looking sloppy . . . even if it was to a bank robbery!

She bounded down the stairs two at a time but came to a stop when she saw Jeremiah looking out from the TV in the family room.

"Hey, Misty," he cried, "what's down?"

"I'd love to talk," she exclaimed, "but I've got to get to the bank robbery!"

"Bank robbery?!"

"Yeah, and Sean may be the robber!"

"What? What's going off?"

"No time. I'll tell you later! See you!"

"But . . . where's your watch? Take your watch so I can come, too!"

Melissa shook her head. "You'd better stay here."

"I want to help!"

Melissa hesitated, then crossed over and patted the top of the TV set as if she were patting the little guy on the head. "Sorry."

"Please . . ." Jeremiah gave his sweetest puppy dog stare topped off with plenty of innocent eye blinking.

"I'd love to take you," she said, "but Larry and

Zomar are going to be there. And the last time you were around those guys, you fell under their spell."

"Take me, take me, take me!"

"Sorry."

Angrily, Jeremiah folded his arms, stomped his foot, and disappeared in a flash of blue.

Melissa turned and raced for the door. But she'd barely stepped outside before she returned and grabbed her handbag.

WEDNESDAY, 22:02 PDST

A crowd had already gathered at the bank by the time Melissa arrived. Mrs. Tubbs was still wearing her purple robe and crown. Mrs. Applewhite was decked out in pink leotards and a matching tutu. Not far away were Bear, Spalding, and KC, along with several other people Melissa didn't recognize.

But she definitely recognized Sean. He was coming out of the bank with a garbage sack full of something.

"Sean!" She raced up to him. "Sean, can you hear me? Sean, it's me, Melissa!"

But he didn't seem to see her.

"Sean!"

Still nothing.

She followed him as he walked to a blue Pontiac

parked in front of the bank and emptied the contents of his sack into the trunk. It was full of money! Hundred-dollar bills, fifties, twenties . . . you name it—if it was money, it was pouring out of his sack and into the trunk!

Mrs. Applewhite was right behind him with another bag full of cash, which she also dumped into the trunk. Suddenly Melissa heard:

"So glad you could join our party."

She spun around to see Larry's smiling face. "Not exactly a trash bag," he said, eyeing Melissa's handbag. "But I guess it'll do. Now, go ahead and join the others. The vault is open, so just go in, fill your bag with money, and dump it into the trunk of my car. Keep doing it until the vault is empty."

Before Melissa could respond, a man came running past them, yelling, "Somebody stop them! They're robbing my bank! Stop them! Stop them!"

It was the bank manager, Mr. Larson.

Larry just laughed. "Yell all you want, old man!" he shouted. "Nobody cares!"

But apparently someone did care. Because at that very moment, a police car roared up, with lights flashing and siren screaming. It screeched to a stop in front of the bank, and Chief Robertson, along with three of his best patrolmen, stepped out . . . just as Spalding exited the bank with a big bag full of cash.

Melissa ran up to the chief. "I'm glad you're here!" she shouted. "Look at this!" She grabbed Spalding's sack and opened it so the policemen could see inside. "These guys are robbing the bank!"

"What are you talking about?" the chief said. He reached into Spalding's sack and pulled out a stack of bills. "What in the—"

"Pie!" Larry shouted.

"COCK-A-DOODLE-DOO!" the chief cried. Suddenly he started pawing at the ground like an overgrown Rhode Island Red. The other policemen followed his lead. One began mooing like a cow, another ran around whinnying like a horse, and the third jumped into the fountain in front of the bank, quacking like a duck and flapping his arms.

Melissa had seen enough. She knew exactly what was going on, and she knew how to stop it. Remembering the word that brought the people out of their trances back at the Comedy Club and later with Jeremiah, she ran up on the bank's steps. "Listen to me, everybody!" she yelled. "Chocolate Cake!"

Immediately, everyone stopped.

"What's going on?" Spalding asked. "What am I doing here?"

Larry ran up onto the steps beside her. "Pie!" he shouted at the top of his lungs.

Immediately, his army of bank robbers went back to work.

Melissa took a breath and shouted, "Chocolate Ca—" until Zomar wrapped his hand around her mouth from behind. But that still didn't stop her. She raised her foot and managed to . . .

CRACK!

. . . get off a good backward kick that nailed him right in the shin.

"OWW!" he screamed, letting her go, hopping up and down on one foot.

Melissa turned and started running down the steps. "Chocolate Cake!" she cried.

"Pie!" Larry shouted.

"Chocolate Cake!"

"Pie!"

"Chocolate Cake!"

By now the "robbers" were stopping and starting, stopping and starting—like so many crazed robots.

"PIE!"

Mrs. Tubbs was headed back into the bank.

"CHOCOLATE CAKE!"

No, she wasn't.

"PIE!"

Yes, she was.

"CHOCOLATE CAKE!"

No, she wasn't.

"PIE!"

Mrs. Applewhite was dancing up a storm.

"CHOCOLATE CAKE!"

Now she wasn't.

"PIE!"

Now she was.

Even Spalding, KC, and Bear were turning and falling over one another, crashing to the ground, getting up, crashing to the ground, getting up. It was like a crazy, mixed-up movie, as if the "robbers" had all short-circuited—going back and forth, spinning around and around as their money flew out of their sacks, hundreds of dollars blowing down the street.

Larry and Zomar could only stare in horror as their "perfect crime" was disintegrating before their very eyes. "PIE!" they both shouted.

"CHOCOLATE—" Suddenly Melissa came to a stop. Staring down the barrel of a .44-caliber magnum will do that to a person. Especially if that .44-caliber magnum is being held by one Zomar the Magnificent.

"I really hope I don't have to use this," he said.

Melissa swallowed hard. "Me too."

"But if you say that word one more time, I shall have to blow you away."

"What word is that?" Melissa asked.

"Chocolate Ca—" Zomar caught himself. "Nice try, kid."

Meanwhile, Larry continued shouting at the crowd. "PIE! PIE! PIE!"

Everyone went back to work, dumping the money into the car while Zomar kept his gun pointed at Melissa.

"You'll never get away with this," she said.

"Oh yes, we will." He flashed her an evil little smile. "Not only that, but your idiot brother over there is going to get all the blame for it."

Melissa's mouth dropped open. "What?"

The smile grew. "The first thing your brother did when he got here was write out a complete confession!" Zomar reached into his pocket, pulled out an envelope, and held it for Melissa to see. It was addressed to the Midvale Police Department, in Sean's handwriting.

Zomar continued. "All I have to do is drop it in the nearest mailbox."

Melissa felt herself starting to panic. "It won't work," she said.

Zomar laughed. "Of course it will work. Take a look around you. Notice anything about all our friends' hands?"

121

Melissa glanced about. "Everyone's wearing gloves," she said.

"That's right. Well, everyone but your brother. His fingerprints are going to be on everything!"

Melissa's panic grew. What could she do? "What about the bank manager?" she demanded. "He's seen everything!"

"No problem," Zomar said. "A quick session with Larry or me, and he won't remember a thing . . . and neither will you."

"What?" Melissa turned back to him. In his free hand he was holding a crystal on a gold chain exactly like Larry had used.

"Just look at this pretty little crystal," he said.

"What are you doing with that?" she demanded.

"Oh, I think you know. Just look at it for a moment."

"No, I—"

"Why resist? No one else is. Just relax. Just close your eyes for a moment."

Already Melissa could feel herself starting to weaken. There was something so soothing about his voice.

"Your eyes, they are growing very heavy. Very, very heavy."

She blinked, trying to keep them open, but he was right—they were getting heavy.

"Don't resist. Come join us. Just close your eyes.

Listen to my voice and close those heavy, heavy eyes."

Well, maybe she would close them. But just for a moment.

"That's a good girl. There you go. Just close them and listen to my—"

"WHAT'S DOWN, DUDS?"

Jeremiah's neurotic voice jarred Melissa awake. It also startled Zomar. The man looked around, trying to find its source. Then he gasped loudly when he looked up to the digital clock and temperature sign above the bank. There was a strange glowing creature with bright red hair . . . and it was staring straight down at him!

"What on Earth?!"

That was all the time Melissa needed to gather her thoughts. With no other weapon but her handbag, she swung it as hard as she could.

WHAP!

She hit Zomar square in the head, instantly sending him into unconsciousness. As he slumped to the sidewalk, he dropped the gun. It clattered down the steps until it was at the feet of Sean, who was carrying another bag of money.

"Sean!" she yelled.

But Larry had seen the gun, too, and was racing for it.

"SEAN!" she cried. "HELP ME! PLEASE HELP ME!"

And then a wonderful thing happened. Even though Sean was still hypnotized, his love for his sister was so strong that he still managed to recognize her voice. Even more important, he realized she was in trouble. He turned to her. He saw her frantically pointing to the gun at his feet. And then he bent down to retrieve it.

At the same exact instant, Larry was also reaching for it, which could only mean . . .

K-BONK!

. . . their heads collided like two freight trains coming from opposite directions!

The good news was Sean's "freight train" was a little harder than Larry's. Ol' Larry dropped to his knees, then collapsed on the steps, joining his partner in the land of unconsciousness. But not Sean. Instead, he grabbed his head. "Ow!" Then he shook it several times, looking around. "Where am I? What happened?"

"Sean!" Melissa cried, running down the steps to join him. "You knocked him out!"

"But why?" Sean asked, looking around, trying to make sense of what he saw. "What happened?"

"I'll tell you in a minute," she answered. "Just help me get these guys tied up before they wake up!"

Still not understanding, but trusting his sister, Sean

nodded numbly. Together they grabbed some spare trash bags and began hog-tying the two men. Then they shoved gags into their mouths so they couldn't say the infamous *p* word.

When they were through, Melissa rose to her feet and was about to shout, "Chocolate Cake" to the crowd one last time when she spotted Jeremiah still up on the digital clock. "Hey, little guy," she grinned. "I owe you."

"Don't mention it." He glanced down, doing his best imitation of a blush. "Like I said, 'A friend in need always gets the worm.'"

And then, *POOF*, just like that, he was gone.

Melissa smiled and turned back to the group. Then she took a deep breath and shouted one last time:

"CHOCOLATE CAKE!"

THURSDAY, 15:30 PDST

The following day, Sean, Melissa, and Slobs joined Herbie and Dad down at the station. They were enjoying the long-delayed yogurt that had been promised.

"Are you sure you're okay?" Melissa asked Herbie.

Their old friend laughed. "I've never been better."

"Really?" Sean asked.

"Absolutely. Go ahead and try me."

"Okay. . . ." Sean glanced at Melissa, who nodded

that she thought it was okay. Then he called out, "Pie!"

All Herbie did was grin. "You see," he said, "I'm still Herbie. Don't even feel like robbing a bank or holding up a stage or anything!"

"That's good," Melissa sighed. "I'm glad that's over with."

"Me too," Herbie agreed. "Thank you, guys. I don't know what would have happened to me if it wasn't for you."

"I do," laughed Sean. "You'd be breaking rocks with a big hammer up at the state penitentiary."

"But one thing still bothers me," Dad said. "How were those guys stealing the money from the comedy club while the place was packed with people?"

"Easy," Sean explained. "They were putting the entire audience into a brief trance, and then—"

"One of them would steal the money," Melissa said.

"And that's how they got Herbie here to steal the money from the school," Sean added. "But then they got greedy and started thinking about the bank."

"And if it wasn't for you two, they might have actually gotten away with it," Dad concluded.

All nodded in silence.

Finally Herbie sighed. "Well, I've certainly learned my lesson," he said.

"About what?" Dad asked.

"About all this reincarnation and past-life stuff. It's a bunch of nonsense."

Melissa nodded. "I just hope everybody else will figure that out, too," she added.

"People will believe whatever they want," Dad said. "Unfortunately, it doesn't always matter if it's the truth or not. Still, I think some of the folks around town are starting to get the picture."

"What do you mean?" Sean asked.

"On my way to the station this morning, I saw a big purple robe sitting in the trash in front of Mrs. Tubbs' house. Looks like she figured it out."

"All right!" Sean and Melissa exchanged high fives.

"I just wonder what you two are going to be up to next," Herbie said.

Dad shook his head. "With Bloodhounds, Inc., I'm afraid there's no telling. I do know one thing, though." He looked to both of his kids with a twinkle.

"What's that?" Melissa asked.

"Whatever it is, it's not going to be boring!"

"When you're right, you're right," Sean said, digging into his yogurt.

"Amen," Melissa agreed.

"Roow-oow-oow . . ." Slobs agreed.

As the dog howled, everyone broke into laughter. Because like it or not, they all knew that it was going to be the truth.

By Bill Myers

Children's Series:
Bloodhounds, Inc. — mystery/comedy
Journeys to Fayrah — fantasy/allegorical
McGee and Me! — book and video
The Incredible Worlds of Wally McDoogle — comedy

Teen Series:
Forbidden Doors

Adult Novels:
Blood of Heaven
Threshold
Fire of Heaven

Nonfiction:
Christ B.C.
The Dark Side of the Supernatural
Hot Topics, Tough Questions